# THE MARRIAGE CHRONICLES

## LYNN BROOKDALE

*Welcome, Brides (and Grooms)-to-be! We are excited that you chose our site to blog about your upcoming wedding! Please note, this site can be made public to share your wedding bliss from the beginning or kept private until you are ready to share your experience with your fellow brides, as well as your family and friends.*

*On this site you will find resources to address all the major wedding topics: securing local vendors, choosing a honeymoon spot, saving money with DIYs, chat rooms to network with other couples for support, and our favorite: The Bride-to-be online journal!*

*Before you begin, please take a few minutes to fill out the form below. Once you have completed the populated fields, a personalized link will be sent to your email address. This link can be shared with your family and friends once you choose to make your site public.*

*Congratulations, Bride-to-be! We thank you again for choosing Weddingbliss.com for your wedding needs and for allowing us to be part of your most intimate day!*

**Bride-to-be Name:** Bethany
**Partner's Name:** Seth
**Wedding Date:** 10-28-17
**Wedding Location:** Heinz Field
**Wedding Theme:** TBD
**Email address:** BBowers@gmail.com

*Yes! I am interested in receiving future newsletters from www.weddingbliss.com*

√ ***No,*** *I am not interested in receiving future newsletters from www.weddingbliss.com*

*The Marriage Chronicles*

## Chapter 1

*Oh my god, it's really happening!* I stood frozen at the altar in my beautiful cream-colored, crystal-encrusted vintage wedding dress, inspired by Daisy Buchanan (circa *The Great Gatsby* era), as the world around me swirled in chaos. I vaguely heard our priest, Father Mel, murmuring to our guests to stay calm; although, he didn't look very calm himself. My mother and father were already taking charge and barking out orders. Someone yelled to call 9-1-1, and I heard a loud sob and was surprised to realize it came from me. I finally looked over to see Seth, my husband-to-be, lying peacefully on the church floor next to me in his crisp black tux . . . passed out. Seriously?!

A few feet over I saw Ellie, my brother's fiancée, in her overly form-fitting-for-nine-months, lacy, champagne-colored bridesmaid dress, about to give birth. *She cannot give birth today! This is my wedding day!* I had spent the last two years planning everything, down to the drink napkins, especially since most of that time was spent in-between steady jobs, thanks to TPR, my last long-term employer, who fired me. (More on them later.) I resisted the urge to scream because I wasn't sure if I'd be able to stop. Instead, I bent down and gently slapped Seth to wake him. I wasn't going through this alone! In the distance I heard faint sirens and prayed to the heavens above that they were coming here to Our Lady of Perpetual Sorrows Catholic Church.

Everything seemed to be happening in slow motion, even though in reality things were happening by the nanosecond. I was about to punch Seth to fully wake him, as he was still mumbling, "I do, Father Hell," but still refused to fully become conscious. Part of me wondered if he was faking at this point. I mean, how the heck does someone stay passed out with constant screaming and over a hundred people bustling about? I was loosening my arm to wind up for a sucker punch when I saw Heidi, one of my best friends and partner in crime, running over to embrace me.

Heidi Ponicki was a firecracker, to say the least. We first met when I started at my old job three years ago at TPR— The Pelligrino Recruiters, which was located in Pittsburgh, our hometown. Heidi was a senior recruiter and took me under her wing while I flailed about, trying to make sense of my role as a recruiter in an extremely dysfunctional office setting. She left before I was fired in the most brutal and unfair way, but we've remained friends ever since. I was glad to have her on my side (as opposed to being her enemy), that's for sure! Heidi had no fear. Everything about her was dark and intimidating—hair, eyes, complexion—which screamed "Italian" from miles away. Her husband Colin was quite the opposite, with his calm demeanor and strong Polish roots. Together they were a riot.

"Calm down there, killer." Heidi laughed in my ear as I lowered my arm, ready to pulverize my soon-to-be-husband from his slumber.

She looked gorgeous in her champagne bridesmaid dress that she had helped me pick out. It didn't hurt that her dark complexion complemented the dress color and did the exact opposite for Ellie. Then again, Heidi could wear a garbage bag and make it look good. I envied her confidence and her slender build, all 5'7" of her.

If anyone could take control of a situation, it was Heidi.

"How is this happening?" I frantically shook my friend, trying to regain my composure. *Breathe, Bethany. 1 . . . 2 . . . 3 . . . Breathe.* I tried to calm myself with breathing exercises I'd once seen on an infomercial. Heidi forced me to sit on a nearby pew, and I let her take control of the situation.

"I don't think she's really in labor. It's those Braxton Hicks contractions. One of your guests on Seth's side is a nurse, so I overheard 'something, something, Braxton' as I was making my way over to you."

Heidi sat down next to me and wrapped her arm around my shoulders. A minute later I felt something cold pressing into my hands. It was a mini flask. *Only Heidi!*

"This is why we are best friends." I laughed and carefully took a small sip of the strong liquor, which immediately hit my stomach and warmed it throughout. Enjoying the sensation, I took another sip—much bigger this time— before passing it back to its rightful owner.

"In times of need, whisky is a girl's best friend." Heidi laughed and smuggled the half-empty flask back into her small, crystal-encrusted carry-on clutch. "C'mon, Bride, let's get you married." Heidi held out her perfectly manicured hand, which I accepted with a scowl.

"But I can't get married. Everything is ruined. Seth is unconscious, and Ellie is giving birth!" I cried out as Heidi held my hand and firmly walked me back over to the altar. I tried to pull myself away, but Heidi was forcefully pulling me along. When I tried to get her attention by yelling at her to stop, my voice wouldn't come. Panic officially set in. The sirens from the ambulance blared and continued to get louder, but I didn't see any paramedics making their way into the church. I looked around in a further state of shock and confusion.

In the far corner, Ellie was laughing and holding her new bundle of joy, and my parents were cooing and introducing everyone to the baby. An actual receiving line had formed! I turned to my right and saw Seth with his tie loosened, laughing and playing cards with Father Mel. *What in the world is going on? This has to be a dream!* I started to pinch myself, but then the sirens got louder and louder. No one else seemed to hear them but me. They became so loud I couldn't hear myself think. My head was pounding. *Make it stop. Make it all stop!*

"Bethany, wake up!" I could hear Seth's voice in the distance, still paired with the sirens, only they had dulled to a low buzz. I squinted as my focus came and went, then smacked my dry lips to erase the feeling of hundreds of cotton balls in my mouth.


MY BODY TREMBLED, and the room began to spin around me. I was having an anxiety attack—on my wedding day! Soon the voices morphed into one long, deep vowel and my vision started to waiver again. *I knew I should have taken my anxiety meds this morning!*

"Bethany, c'mon, wake up, babe!" I heard Seth's gentle voice again, this time it seemed much closer. His warm breath washed over me like waves on a shore. The scary, deep echo of voices sounded farther away now. I drew in a deep breath and blinked one eye open, unsure of what to expect in my view.

I propped myself up on one elbow while I waited for my world to make sense. After two blinks, I dug a glob of sleep crust from my right eye and suddenly recognized the black and yellow comforter draped over me.

A wave of relief rushed through my body. *It was all a nightmare!* We had two months left before our wedding, and I was starting to come undone. Taking a moment to look around, I realized I was still in my own bed, well, one I shared with my fiancé Seth. After realizing I had been asleep and dreamt the whole debacle, I gasped and jumped up from my side of the bed as Seth stared up at me. The sirens were my annoying alarm clock in full throttle, which I was always responsible for turning off yet somehow slept through.

So, there was no baby . . . yet. I blew out a huge sigh of relief.

Seth looked at me like I had five heads. It was just a silly dream. I'd chalk it up to wedding jitters, nothing to worry Seth or myself about. I made a mental note to check the wedding website I was using to see if this was a normal occurrence for other brides-to-be.

*Act normal, Bethany. Don't freak him out!* I let out a strangled laugh that sounded like a dying cat and tried to shake off the nightmare. Seth stared at me with crooked brows.

"Umm — are you okay? I've never seen you thrash around in your sleep before." He scrutinized me from the other side of the bed.

I cleared my throat and gave him my best *before-seven-AM* smile I could muster.

"I'm good. Just a crazy dream. Can't even remember it now." I laughed and lay back down on our bed, hoping no further explanation was needed. My heart still thumped a mile a minute.

Seth chuckled and stretched his hands over his head while still in bed. "Oh yeah, I always have those deranged dreams where I come home and we have three crazy kids running around." He chuckled and winked at me.

*And how is that a nightmare?!*

Satisfied that I was okay, Seth leaned down and gave me a quick peck on the cheek before he jumped out of bed to start his day. My fiancé was a creature of habit. I could recite his morning routine with my eyes closed. Like clockwork, as he walked out of the bedroom, he stretched his hands over his head again and let out a long, agonizing yawn — and for good measure, he cracked his knuckles twice before he headed towards the bathroom to get ready. He seemed oblivious as I lay there still in a distant daze.

"I need to jump in the shower. I've got an early day at work. We're getting trained on a new device we're rolling out." He nonchalantly announced his morning plans as he halfway disappeared around the corner. He constantly did that, and it drove me crazy. He would start talking to me after he'd left the bedroom, and half the time I couldn't make sense of anything he said. Sometimes I would hear him calling my name from the bathroom, and when I would peek my head in to see what he wanted, he would stare at me, waiting for an answer to something he thought I could hear from another room. No matter how many times I asked him to talk to me when we were both in the same room, he never seemed to remember that request.

Daily Deliveries was a local telephone service provider where Seth had been working for over five years. We first met when I was hired at Teleport, a life insurance telemarketing job. I was required to make at least a dozen cold calls per hour and try to sell life insurance to unsuspecting senior citizens. Seth's job was to deliver phone equipment to our office whenever a new employee started or when we needed upgrades.

At first we exchanged simple smiles and greetings, then we slowly became acquaintances, until he finally asked me out on a date. From that moment on, we were inseparable. He was the yin to my yang. After a few dates, I knew he was the one for me, and on our one-year anniversary he proposed to me after we left Primanti Brothers—an amazing and historic sandwich shop located in Market Square.

We had a great lunch date where we bonded over their famous Pitts-burger and cheese sandwiches, which were loaded high with homemade fries, coleslaw, and tomatoes. I was full after only eating half of my sandwich, but to waste such a creation would have been a sin, so I continued to shovel pieces of sandwich into my mouth until my stomach refused to accept any more. Seth had devoured his same sandwich in under ten bites and spent the rest of the time staring longingly at my poorly eaten one, like a puppy waiting for scraps. I finally gave in and let him finish what I couldn't. As we left the restaurant, Seth grabbed my arm lightly and stopped us both in our tracks. "Hold on, I have to tie my shoe," he said.

I froze. I knew Seth always double-knotted his shoes. My heart skipped a beat. *Oh my god, is this really happening?* My heart fluttered and I felt a deep blush working its way up my face.

I looked down and saw Seth on one knee. He held up a small black box. "Bethany, this has been the best year of my life. When I'm with you, I'm happier than I've ever been. I want to wake up to your smile every day for the rest of my life. Will you marry me?" It felt like hot coals were sliding down my cheeks, and my heart raced a mile a minute, yet I just knew this was my moment. I had always wanted my Prince Charming to whisper these exact words to me; maybe not while feeling so bloated after eating a thousand calories, but it was close enough to the perfect scenario. Well, perfect enough for Seth. I would have preferred a nice candlelit dinner proposal or something private, like a walk through our favorite park. But I guess the Primanti Brothers' front walkway would do. Regardless, he was asking me to be his wife!

A few pedestrians started clapping and cheering as I shrieked, "Yes!" and threw my arms around Seth. He put the ring on my finger, and I couldn't stop smiling. It was perfect: a vintage design with a round stone and pavé diamonds in the filigree. I immediately fell in love with that ring, its symbol, and everything it would soon stand for. Love. . . and soon to follow. . . marriage. *True commitment.*

We decided on a two-year engagement so we would have time to save up for our wedding. Now here we were, two months until the big day. *Had so much changed since that day at Primanti Brothers, or was I just letting my nerves get to me?*

Against my will I also got out of bed to prepare myself for a full day of work at an independent art museum called the Brick Street Gallery, located in the downtown district. I loved that the building was set back from the main strip, which housed a coffee shop and an independent boutique that carried books and clothes. In the summertime, patrons would browse the bookstore, purchase a latte, and then walk over to the museum to look around. Although it was still a temp-to-hire position, I was grateful to just receive a paycheck. I actually enjoyed the job, even though the pay was much lower than what I made at TPR and I still lacked any benefits of my own. Still, it was a job.

While Seth took a shower, I made my way into the kitchen to start a pot of coffee. I didn't believe in spending a ridiculous amount of money on a machine that was responsible for sputtering out a weak batch of coffee, so I stuck with my handy dandy Mr. Coffee machine, circa 1990. While stores marketed the top-of-the-line Keurig machines that kept outdoing one another every six months and cost an arm and a leg, (not to mention the separate Keurig cups to brew the overpriced coffee), I stuck with my $14.99 old-school coffee maker. It also held special meaning to me since it was my first adult purchase—with my first real paycheck—once I graduated high school and I was trying to rebel against my mother, who only drank tea. I still remember that day she came downstairs and saw me pouring myself a cup of dark-roast Folgers. I thought she would get out her good rosary beads right then and there and pray for my soul. (My parents were devout Catholics and very much against drinking, swearing... you name it and my mother found sin in it somewhere.)

I made a full carafe—my typical routine that carried me through getting ready at the house—then took the rest with me in my worn-out *Duquesne University* travel mug. The letters were barely visible anymore, but it was my favorite mug and I refused to part with it. It was like a ratty old blanket that had no special meaning to anyone other than the child to whom it belonged. I could hear Seth, now in the bedroom, opening and closing dresser drawers. That was my cue to slip into the bathroom while it was free.

Instead of relaxing in the shower, my mind raced. With two months left, I still had a ton of items to check off my "to-do" list that seemed to grow by the minute. We still had to order the wedding cake. Seth and I hadn't reached a compromise on the final flavor and look just yet. If it were up to Seth, he would have a gold cake with black fondant piping and a Pittsburgh flag or emblem etched across it. Every tier would be plain vanilla—his favorite, and my least favorite—cake flavor. Since I desired a more vintage feel to the wedding, I wanted something simple yet elegant. And each tier was to be a different flavor to allow the guests variety. Maybe it would have cascading roses coming down one side of it, and I would incorporate the color ivory. Seth wrinkled his nose at the mention of ivory. "Shouldn't weddings use pure white? Ivory sounds like something my grandma would wear." He ended the conversation there.

Our colors for the wedding were gold and black, since Seth was a die-hard Pittsburgh fan. Our reception was at Heinz Field for this very reason. I was determined, however, to add my vintage vision and not feel like I was walking into a high school prom. Seth wanted balloons, which I vetoed, telling him this was our wedding and not a homecoming dance.

Then there were the invitations, which still needed to be mailed out. I was done patiently waiting on a handful of addresses from Seth's side, and he seemed to keep forgetting to ask his mother for help. *That's it. If I don't get these addresses by the end of the week, then Uncle Fletcher and sweet Aunt Louise are not making the cut.* Feeling better about my decision to be firm, I dried off and got out of the shower. Seth had already left for his early morning meeting, so I had the house to myself, which I couldn't even enjoy since I now had to hustle to get to work as well.

The parking lot was already full when I finally pulled into work. I had to circle the block a few times until I stalked a college kid, who was leaving the coffee shop—latte in one hand, texting on his cell phone with the other. He didn't even bother to look both ways before crossing the main street to get to his car, which was parallel parked on the side street. *Great.*

So far my Monday was off to a great start. First, a massive wedding nightmare which, truthfully, could still legitimately happen. Then the anxiety of my mental "to-do" list that was growing by the minute. And now, parallel parking. This was a sign.

I kept scanning the area in case a better parking spot suddenly opened up, but I was already tight on time, so my options were limited to this tall lanky kid, who seemed to be taking his sweet time. I thought back to when I was a college student and never had time to spare. I was always sprinting from one class to another or accidently oversleeping, which caused me to rush around in haste, never a moment for myself. Not to mention the fact that my mother called me religiously, every night for the whole four weeks I was away at college.

Unfortunately, I figured out I wasn't very keen on having a metal chick for a roommate. She adorned our walls with alternative Jesus posters, yet listened to death metal. The first time I met Claire, she had more metal poking out of her body than anyone I had ever seen. She scared the bejesus out of me with her multiple ear piercings, nose piercing, and tongue ring. I was also dumbfounded by the *I heart Jesus* and *Christ is our Savior* tattoos along her arm, which cascaded down her right wrist. Duquesne University was a Catholic college. I wasn't sure how Claire managed to get in, unless her parents had confused boarding school with higher education. After four weeks I begged my parents to let me commute from home, and only at the mention of "death metal" did my mother wholeheartedly agree that it was for the best, and that both of them would be down the following weekend to help me pack.

This kid, however, seemed to have all the time in the world. Now he was leaning against his driver's side door, sipping his overpriced coffee (How could he afford a $7 latte on a student budget?!), while his other hand was going a mile a minute typing on his phone. I let out a frustrated sigh.

I closed my eyes and tried a two-minute meditation. *Breathe. 1-2-3… Breathe. Repeat.* A minute later I opened my eyes and, thank God, he finally managed to get into his beat up, rusted red Camry and start the engine.

I checked the clock on my dashboard. I still had five minutes to get inside and clock in before I was considered late. I hated being late, especially with a boss like Embeth Findlay. She always acted aloof but, somehow, she always knew when someone was tardy, even when she wasn't onsite. I truly believe she had meticulously placed hidden cameras around the museum for this very reason, unless she really did have eyes in the back of her head—like my mother would always tell us when we were younger and always seemed to know when we were up to no good.

Embeth embodied the essence of having it all without looking like she even had to try. She wore nothing but couture outfits, and I'd yet to see her wear something twice. Laced, beaded, sparkly… you name it, and she owned it. She sported every top-of-the-line piece of fabric and always made it look great, even on her larger frame. Her fine auburn hair was always in a coiffed updo, never down. She had the perfect-sized hazelnut eyes, which always boasted heavy makeup. She looked immaculate any time I saw her, which created a strong layer of confidence that she wore like a badge of honor.

She had this aura about her, like she had traveled the

world yet decided to come back to Pittsburgh instead of somewhere worthy like Paris. She was in her late fifties (I caught a glimpse of her driver's license once), and rumor had it she had taken her ex-husband, *the famous* Brick Findlay, for every penny he was worth. Hence, she inherited the museum he had originally owned. I still had no idea what her backstory was, and no one seemed particularly inclined to tell me, so I just created different scenarios in my head. *She caught him in bed with another woman. Or man? He was cheating on her with a young, hot blonde and got busted. He filed for divorce after seeing her credit card statements.* Heidi and I sometimes made up these funny, outrageous stories about both of our managers while we bonded over glasses of wine at our trademark spot, Happy Hour.

Embeth was the female version of Topher, my old supervisor from TPR. Except, where he was hyper and obnoxious, she was more laid back about getting her point across. More passive-aggressive, one might say. She had a way of making you feel bad if you didn't want to do something, such as stay late on short notice. One day she came around and casually told everyone that we had a potential exhibitor interested in us and that we had to showcase our very best pieces of art so we would get the bid and outshine our competitor. She then casually mentioned that we should start dusting, organizing, and sweeping . . . before they arrived to scope out the place. It was a quarter to five at this point— fifteen minutes before closing time— and the three of us who were still on the clock raced around to get all the chores done, with the hope that this would be considered overtime. Of course, it never was, as this was always a "last-minute favor" that we were doing for her.

Embeth always over exaggerated things, so when someone did speak up (very seldom anymore) to announce his or her schedule conflicts in staying late, Embeth would automatically rearrange her painted-on face. Her perfectly plump lips, probably full from monthly lip injections, would turn into the most perfect pout, accompanied by a dramatic sigh. "I know it's last minute, and I am *soooo* sorry, but this just came about, and I couldn't possibly do it all myself in time." She would fake an apology and then stare us down, batting her phony lashes at us until we all murmured, "Sure" or "I understand, no problem." Then she would whisk herself away to her office or simply disappear without a word. I was too scared to ever voice my opinion, so I just accepted her orders and turned into Cinderella whenever she asked.

Of course, my annoying co-worker, Kendall, was already manning the front desk when I walked in. Today she had on a bright-pink pantsuit and a thick, gold, knotted necklace to emphasize her large chest. Her overdyed blonde hair had been pulled up into a high bun, and she already had slight perspiration forming around the sides of her forehead even though the air conditioning was on. I could hear her typing away with her fake press-on nails, which she probably had painted to match her outfit. I had no idea why she always dressed up on Monday, since the museum was closed. Kendall always outdid me in the clothes, makeup, and hair department. I picked a piece of invisible lint off the front of my white t-shirt, which was also a bit wrinkled, and noticed an empty Starbucks cup shoved in the corner of the small desk.

"Heeey, Beth." Kendall stopped typing when she saw me walk by. I forced a smile as I set my purse down behind her desk. "Hey, Kendall. How was your weekend?" I cringed after the words left my mouth, knowing this would be a full-blown twenty-minute account of her entire life story. She moved over so I could clock in on the only computer we had up front. Kendall rolled her eyes and sighed dramatically. *Oh boy . . . here we go!* I should have waited until I grabbed a cup of coffee from the break room before I even asked.

"Well, Saturday, Nolin was supposed to swing by and get the boys, but he never showed." Nolin was the ex-husband, and they shared custody of their seven-year-old twin boys. Kendall shook her head in dismay, along with another eye roll, and continued. "I mean, it's one thing to hurt my feelings, but it's not right to hurt the boys. So, of course, I had to make up an excuse when he never showed up to take them." I nodded my head to show I was listening. She continued, "Grant and Grayson don't deserve that, you know? I mean, I'm sure he was with that tramp!" Kendall's face flushed when she said the word "*tramp,*" but she regained composure and kept talking.

"I don't know what he sees in her! I mean, she could be his daughter for heaven's sake!" Nolin was pushing forty and apparently was having an early mid-life crisis with a woman half his age. Kendall, who was a few years younger than him, immediately kicked him out of their house when she came across a pair of panties wadded up in his Docker pants on laundry day. I still remembered her telling me this horrific and very personal story when I had only been employed at the museum for a few weeks. "Black-laced, practically see-through thongs! What type of woman wears such a thing?" She had confided in me when we were alone up front, when she was supposed to be training me, not bearing her soul to a complete stranger!

I nodded and shrugged at all the appropriate times until the phone rang, which saved me. I waited until Kendall slipped on her headphones (Why couldn't she just pick up the actual phone?) and began chatting with the person on the other end before I slipped out back for my morning cup of coffee.

The day flew by. I enjoyed being closed on Mondays. We were just there catching up on work. I had a small project to finish up, which was to create a spreadsheet of attendance rates and donors' monetary contributions from one of our larger exhibits earlier that month. I had the process down pat now, considering it was the reason Embeth hired me to begin with.

Five o'clock snuck up on me, as I had been holed up in Embeth's office practically all day. I was a bit surprised she wasn't in at all, considering she liked to walk around and make sure we were always busy, opting to find us something to clean if we didn't appear productive. She was probably out pampering herself for a day—spa, hair, nails, and an extravagant lunch, of course. I'd overheard many phone conversations where Embeth was out somewhere on her "pamper day" and called in to have Kendall order her favorite sushi dish to be delivered to wherever she was—usually her uppity hair salon downtown. I once looked up their website and balked at the prices. A haircut alone would set me back one month's pay, yet Embeth religiously had appointments every four to six weeks.

I was in my car by quarter after and got home to see Seth's car already in the driveway. It was then that I remembered he had gone in early for a meeting. I made my way to the back door, pondering what to make for dinner.

I walked in to smell—and see—Angelo's pizza on the table and Seth already digging into a slice of extra-cheese pizza. I smiled, thankful I didn't have to make dinner for one night. Not to mention it was about eighty-five degrees out, and I hated to cook on those days. "I love you."

I set my purse down on the counter and opened a bottle of wine before joining Seth at the table. It was the perfect ending to a halfway-decent day aside from the fact that he, once again, forgot to put any toppings on my pizza. I mean, would it kill the guy to ask them to throw a few mushrooms on my side? *Plain cheese. Always plain cheese.* I sighed and then finagled a slice of pizza onto my dish, followed by a sip of wine. "How was your day, babe?"

This was our usual chit chat after work. I would ask about his day, and he would reply with a few words, then I would launch into a whole spiel about Kendall and her new crazy drama for the week. Sometimes (most days) it was a mix of her and Embeth.

After dinner I retreated to the living room to surf through

TV channels. It was Seth's turn to do the dishes, for which I was grateful—even though that's probably why he ordered pizza. My eyes were glued to the screen as a kangaroo was giving birth on Animal Planet, until my phone dinged. It was Heidi. *Saved by the bell.*

## Chapter 2

*I Have BIG News!*

I read Heidi's text and immediately responded:

*Are you pregnant?!*

That was always my first guess. She told me that she and Colin were going to start trying again this year. Heidi found out she had an ectopic pregnancy the previous year and refused to try again for quite some time, so it was exciting that she was ready and willing now.

*Not yet … I'm moving!*

*Where? Did you find a house over in that development you liked?*

Colin and Heidi were currently living in a townhouse, and Heidi had been pleading with him for months to upgrade to a house. Especially if they were to get pregnant, they needed more room. She started randomly looking around the area and found a few nice houses online that she showed me a few weeks ago.

Two minutes later, another beep.

*Not exactly. We're moving to... Cleveland! Long story. Don't hate me.*

Wait. What? Did I read that correctly? *Crap.* No. This was worse than crap. This was a shut-the-front-door moment.

I stared in horror at the text from Heidi. *"We're moving to Cleveland."* the words glared at me from my screen as if at any minute they might come alive and attack me. *How can this be happening?* I couldn't lose my best friend to another state, especially right before my wedding! Why did the universe hate me? My fingers moved at the speed of lightning: *I'm calling you right now!*

Heidi launched into an apology the second she answered my call, "I'm so sorry. I literally just found out at dinner tonight."

Twenty minutes later and half a bottle of wine polished off, I finally spoke up and decided not to turn into Bridezilla and flood her with guilt of leaving before my wedding day. She was my Maid of Honor, but I would deal with that later. I decided to play the supportive friend role and would later cry and complain to Seth about everything. That's what fiancés are for, right?

"Well, Josie is going to flip out when you tell her you're quitting your job to move to Cleveland." I smirked, knowing that she would enjoy nothing more than telling her egotistical manager she was giving her notice. Thankfully, Colin made a good enough salary that she could afford to not work for a few months in Cleveland. Being the regional supervisor for a very well-to-do national security firm had its perks. I tried to use my peppiest voice and pretend that I was happy for her.

Heidi groaned on the other end of the line. "I'm so sorry, Bethany. I know the timing is awful, but this came as a total surprise to me too! We had no idea that Colin's great aunt put her house in his name to inherit after her passing. Apparently, death isn't keen on keeping up with social calendars. But yeah, Josie is going to flip her shit." I could tell Heidi was grinning when she mentioned her nightmare of a boss.

I knew she was trying to make me laugh and keep me from having a breakdown. I also knew it wasn't her fault that

Colin's great aunt (and godmother) had suddenly passed from a freak stroke at the age of sixty-five and had left the house in his name. Evidently, they were very close, and she wanted to keep the house in the Ponicki name and not have some random stranger living in it. Fair enough. But did it need to be in Cleveland?

After Heidi promised to be present for any upcoming wedding plans, as long as I could give her a week's notice so she could travel back and forth, I filled her in on Kendall's latest drama. We made small talk for a few minutes before hanging up.

I tossed my phone onto my bed and began watching my show, wine in hand—my typical Monday night routine. I have a serious addiction to everything on Bravo. *The Real Housewives of New York, Beverly Hills, Orange County.* You name it . . . I watch it. Tonight, I was catching up on the *RHONY,* my personal favorite, if I had to pick one. I was just getting into the whole John and Bethenny debacle (Dorinda's boyfriend whom no one liked) at the lingerie party when my phone beeped. It was a text from my brother, reminding me of the dress fitting for Ellie's wedding after work on Wednesday. I groaned and tossed the phone back onto my bed after confirming that yes, I would be there; and no, I didn't forget. Ugh, I wished I could forget about that wedding altogether. No such luck.

Thirty minutes later I gave up on watching my shows. My heart wasn't in it after finding out that Heidi was moving out of state, and right before my wedding. I tried to talk to Seth about it, but he was deeply involved in some documentary about the Pittsburgh Steelers on ESPN, and all I got from him was a limp pat to my back and him grumbling something about her moving to a city where their football team would never see the Super Bowl. Real encouraging.

I decided to power up my laptop and do some online journaling. Maybe it would de-stress me. Imagine if Kate Spade and David Tutera took over Pinterest. That was the concept of Weddingbliss.com. It was just as addicting, except you could also journal your wedding experience from start to finish. I was using the journal section as free therapy since I didn't have insurance to cover a real therapist yet. I'd yet to set my profile as public, but I had fun scrolling through other brides' open posts. I just didn't have the nerve to do the same yet. I entered the website address in the browser and hit enter.

www.weddingbliss.com

**Welcome back, Bethany! Would you like to continue where you left off?**

**Great! Have fun journaling!**

I began typing as soon as the cursor appeared.

*I just found out my MOH is moving. . . to another state! She promises to still do her MOH duties, but how is that possible when she will only be around on weekends?! Once Seth tells his mom, I know that my soon-to-be mother-in-law will want to swoop in and try to take charge —aka plan my wedding the way she wants it. I can just hear her now, "Oh, Beth dear, are you sure those are the napkin colors you want to go with? Why don't you look at a few options I picked out?" Then Seth will encourage all her choices and I will be left looking like a bridezilla if I don't comply. It's bad enough that my parents already have a huge say in our big day—mostly because they are fronting a big portion of our bill. Unlike Josh and Ellie, my parents are basically forcing us to get married in a church, opposed to having everything on-site at Heinz Field like Seth and I originally planned. Why are our parents still running our lives? Argh.*

*Seriously, why does the universe hate me? I also gained two pounds this week. I can't even blame it on Heidi's moving announcement, but I'm sure that will add another pound or two of unwanted cellulitis to my waistline by Friday. Can stress make you gain weight? Maybe I should try my wedding dress on again for safe measure. Although, I'm not sure if Vera, my wedding seamstress, would be happy to see my face again! Aren't they used to anxious brides wanting to try their dresses on multiple times a week? I didn't think the request was being obnoxious, but I have noticed that lately all my calls go right to her voicemail. Hmm. Okay, so maybe questioning her alteration skills was a mistake, but I swear the waistline was looser when I tried it on the previous week. Getting married is more stressful than taking the SATs.*

# Chapter 3

My brother Josh and his pregnant fiancée Ellie were getting married at the end of the month. In hindsight I was grateful that we ended up pushing our wedding back until October, even though I wasn't happy she was stealing my thunder and getting married first.

I didn't like Ellie McPherson. She made me feel insecure … with her perfect body, thick blond hair, and crisp blue eyes. She could substitute as a Victoria's Secret runway model, and she was now going to be my sister-in-law. Josh constantly bragged that people came up to her and asked if she was Gisele Bundchen. It was hard not to roll my eyes, especially after hearing the same story for the fifteenth time.

Ellie was a college dropout whose parents were well off, so holding a job wasn't a priority. Josh ran into her one day at a nearby coffee shop that was close to his office downtown. Turned out, she had an addiction to caffeine and was standing in line ordering a Skinny Vanilla Latte—just before her monthly shopping spree—when Josh walked in. I had their love story memorized by now, and it was hard not to gag every time Josh told it.

"I walked in and there she was—the most gorgeous girl I had ever seen, standing in front of me."

At this point of the story, Josh would look over at Ellie and smile like a fool. Ellie would bat her eyes (fake lashes, of course) and laugh out loud as she squeezed his hand for him to continue. She ate up the attention with a flavor spoon.

Josh would go on to explain how he tapped her on the shoulder and asked for her number - after gushing and telling her that she was the most beautiful girl he had ever laid eyes on, and that he would be honored to take her out to dinner . . . if she didn't have a boyfriend, of course! *Typical Josh, always going above and beyond.*

At this point Ellie would jump in and finish the story from her point of view. "He was drop-dead gorgeous, so, of course I accepted!" She would go on "...I mean, I had just broken up with my pre-law boyfriend, so I took it as a sign when I ran into Josh that day."

Everyone would *ooh* and *ahh* then smile at the happy couple. Everyone except me, of course.

On Wednesday, my mother called me on my lunch break to remind me that I was to meet them at the bridal-and-alterations shop after work. Ellie was having her final dress fitting, and I needed to go try on my ridiculous bridesmaid dress, too. First off, a bridesmaid dress should *not* cost more than a mortgage payment. Secondly, it should not pay homage to the short-lived Kim Kardashian and Kris Humphries wedding—unless Josh would experience wedded bliss for all of seventy-two days before a nasty divorce! Ellie was obsessed with the Kardashian women —specifically Kim, the queen of fashion. So, she had spent an ungodly number of hours trying to recreate Kim's first wedding, which she called a "classic fairytale." Clearly, she was confusing an icon like Princess Diana, with a *wanna be* like Kim Kardashian. I huffed at the price tag when I first saw the brides-maid dress that Ellie had pointed out to me on our first gathering.

I believe my mouth fell open, and I was waiting for my mother to laugh it off and say they were just pulling my leg. Instead they all stared at me, expectantly, waiting for me to smile and agree that the dress was perfect. It was a white mermaid-style dress that fluffed out at the bottom with feathers. I was horrified.

The first time we all met up at the couture bridal shop, I was taken aback at how ritzy and glamorous everything was. We were on the east side of town in an area known as Shady Side—a location I rarely frequented unless we were passing by on a detour. It was a historic portion of Pittsburg boasting upscale homes, stores, and restaurants. Residents and shoppers entered and exited from cars that cost more than our house. I watched as mothers walked with their young daughters along the sidewalk leading up to five-star restaurants to have lunch. Seth and I had never even fathomed such a treat. We got excited if we could use a coupon at the end of our meal. Not only did we have a wedding to save for, but we both didn't come close to the salary that my brother made, so we had to pinch every penny just to stay afloat.

I also noticed that my mother was wearing her best church outfit, complete with her good pearls, for the occasion. Yet she wore plaid pedal pushers at my dress fitting, complete with her gardening flip flops. When I grumbled about her looking better for Ellie's benefit, she threw her hands up in exasperation and stared pointedly at me, daring me to say more. *Oh no. Here it comes. I walked myself right into one of her "we treat you and your brother fairly" speeches.* As if reading my mind, she stood up a little straighter and brought her shoulders back, before wiggling her pointer finger at me. "You know your father and I do not play favorites, young lady. I looked just fine at your dress fitting. Besides, God doesn't care about looks or material things. Remember that. Which reminds me, have you gone to see Father Mel in a while?" My mother always managed to lecture Josh and me every Sunday following mass after being disappointed when neither of us bothered to show up and fill the two spots she always reserved next to her in the third pew back from the altar.

*Oh, great! I'm back to being lectured about church.* Father Mel was fresh off the boat from Ireland. We guessed that he must have had an end-of-life crisis when he decided to emigrate to the U.S. because he must've been at least eighty when we started school, which would make him now over a hundred years old. His nickname at the elementary school was "Father Hell," and by the time we were in high school and had taken Greek and Latin classes, we called him "Father Melancholia." Father Hell never smiled, and he spoke in a monotonous voice, which would be difficult to do with an Irish accent. You could never tell if he was happy or sad, tired, or mad, because he only had one mood: Catholic. Last Christmas Eve, my mother invited him over, and he proceeded to drink all the liquor I had brought with me in retaliation to my parents putting Ellie—who didn't even show up—ahead of their own daughter.

When would Josh tell my mother about Ellie's stance on religion? The thought made me smile like the Grinch.

It was June when we had first met up at the couture bridal shop, when Ellie screeched excitedly over the phone to my mother that she had found *The Dress!* The next day we all gathered around, ready to witness *The Dress.* Ellie's parents were still vacationing in France, so Josh had asked my mother ahead of time to step in and be there for Ellie. Apparently, she needed a mother figure to share this moment with and, of course, my mother ate it up. She would do anything for her soon-to-be daughter-in-law, carrying her soon-to-be grand-baby, which was already making an appearance on Ellie's thin frame.

Even though Josh swore he loved Ellie, I still wondered if this was a sham and he proposed because she had gotten pregnant. Josh held himself to high standards, but he never talked about getting married and having children. That was my dream. He just wanted the white picket fence and big house.

Once again he seemed to be getting it all and then some, while I was still trying to win my debate with Seth on having a *planned* baby and starting a family - something he had no interest in.

The first time I saw Ellie's wedding dress, I literally stopped breathing. I was beyond amazed that anyone could look so beautiful. It truly was breathtaking but, of course, I didn't tell her that. Ellie had found a similar Vera Wang ball gown that mirrored the exact look of the one Kim Kardashian wore years before, maybe even better. It was pure white and had a poofy-yet-delicate tulle that sparkled from the waist down. The top portion was a slight sweetheart shape that was dusted in fine crystals so that it almost glowed in the light. It was gorgeous. I had to give her credit. She had found the mother of all dresses.

Ellie was staying true to her vision and replicating the diva's reception of a black-tie affair, minus the million-dollar budget. Josh was adamant that he was on board with this plan and even encouraged Ellie to do whatever her heart desired. *Who is this guy, and what did he do with my brother?*

Apparently, he was happily scouting prices for a cigar bar, whatever that meant. I knew that Josh made good money and that the word "budget" wasn't really in Ellie's and his vocabulary, especially since her parents were extremely well off. Must be nice to have your dream wedding and lack the stress of funding it. Meanwhile, I did have a budget and I was not "living the dream" by any means.

During our final dress fitting on Wednesday, I grudgingly took the white mermaid dress and obediently tried it on in a dressing room that was larger than my current bedroom—perhaps even my house! I gasped as I walked into one of the three designer dressing rooms that were located in the back of the store. Upon entering, I noticed two large white, pristine sitting chairs, a glass table that matched a larger coffee table along the shorter of the four walls, and a mirror that ran from floor to ceiling in the center of the room. Then, there were two sets of standing mirrors that connected to three sides, so anyone in a garment could get a three-dimensional look of the overpriced dress they were modeling. There were two garment racks with hangers along the middle of the room, and then an alteration station set up in the far back corner. I could almost fit our whole house into this one room!

I stepped into the dress and immediately felt like I was suffocating in the skin-tight tulle material that clung to my body like saran wrap. I'm not sure why anyone thought a mermaid-style dress was suitable for a wedding. It felt like being bound together with duct tape at my ankles and I had to waddle my way over to the door, almost tripping over my own two feet in the process. It looked like I had a dozen dead birds trailing me at the bottom of my dress. Whose idea was it to add umpteen million bird feathers from the knees down on a dress? How in the world is this stylish? *I'm a walking decoy,* I thought to myself.

I opened the dressing room door and watched as my mother, Ellie, Jasmine and Claudia—her two other brides-maids—smiled as I walked out. Ellie held up a pair of white, four-inch heeled, rhinestone-covered shoes and handed them to me. *You have GOT to be kidding me!*

"The shoes are my treat. I found them last week, and I thought they would go perfectly with your dress! Your mom told me you were a size eight, so these should fit." Ellie smiled brightly, showing off her perfectly straight and white teeth, as she held up the shoes—proud of her accomplishment to secretly break my ankles.

I glared at my mother, who didn't seem to notice, as Ellie excitedly handed them over to me then directed her other two bridesmaids to change into their dresses so she could take a picture of her "three gorgeous girls," as she put it.

I sat down on a white satin bench located directly outside of the dressing room and tried to slip on my new and unwanted stripper shoes. *Josh owes me big time!* I didn't even want to be in this wedding, but he basically guilted me into it. He said that Ellie would be heartbroken if I declined. *Yeah right.*

These heels were the most uncomfortable footwear I had ever forced my feet into. I could already feel the blisters forming. When I tried to stand, laser-sharp pain shot through my feet. I was afraid I'd have welts the minute I removed them.

Ellie rounded the corner and shrieked when she saw me in them. "Oh, Bethany, those look amazzz-ing!" She clapped her hands together, and I wondered if she genuinely enjoyed seeing me in pain.

I forced a tight smile and immediately tried to sit back down and remove the razors from my poor innocent feet, which were now tingling.

My mother, who was oblivious to my pain at this point, fumbled for her disposable camera in her purse. They still made those?! My parents refused to get in touch with reality and own cell phones. They didn't believe in technology that surpassed the year 1990.

"Bethany, let me get a picture of you. Stand back up." My mother directed me back over to the middle of the room. Today was pure torture. I groaned and obeyed. At this point my feet were beyond help anyway. I saw a soaking bath in my near future.

My mother snapped about a dozen photos—some with me alone and some with Ellie, who, at six-months pregnant, was still skinnier than me. Ellie wore a sleek black Dolce & Gabbana pantsuit, complete with black, open-toe heels that made her tower over me without shoes on. Diamond-studded, silver bracelets adorned her right arm. Her two-carat engagement ring sparkled on her ring finger and almost made her hand look miniature.

I was stuck in a three-ring circus. I hated Kim Kardashian at this point and vowed that if I ever met her, I would berate her for having such an elaborate first wedding and ruining my life in the process. I had googled the Kardashian wedding ahead of time, so I was prepared for what my dress would look like, but nothing could prepare me for the reality of trying it on. Of course, all the Kardashian sisters looked good in their mermaid-style dresses. They were probably all airbrushed for the magazines.

Jasmine and Claudia stepped out of the dressing room looking stunning in the very same dress that I felt claustrophobic and restrained in—and to add insult to injury—seemed to move their bottom torsos freely with no issues. Was I in the twilight zone? My mother gasped and once again pulled out her ancient portable camera and began taking more photos while simultaneously mumbling words like "gorgeous" and "just stunning" to herself—even though I was close enough to hear.

# Chapter 4

Heidi and I frequented this sleek, modern bar called Happy Hour where we spent endless hours gossiping and catching up —men free—at least once a week. As I walked in, I saw one of my favorite servers making his way to the hostess area. He recognized me and smiled as he waved. Preston had gotten to know Heidi and me fairly well, especially last year when we basically lived here during our time working at TPR and consuming one too many cocktails while having a bitch fest over Topher—the ringleader—and the rest of the circus we were forced to call our co-workers.

I picked at my nail as I casually took in my surroundings and waited for Preston to make his way to the hostess stand. The wine bar had undergone a full renovation at the end of last year. The owner decided the entire venue needed an update. With its lofty skylight ceilings and beautiful soft tones, one couldn't help but feel immediately welcomed by the sleek, wraparound ebony bar in the middle of the room and mid-century modern marble communal tables scattered about. The look was completed by a few high-top tables lining one side of the back wall. Artwork donated from talented artists enrolled in the community college around the corner, adorned the walls and encompassed the venue's contemporary style.

"Preston, how are you?" I smiled as the older gentleman appeared next to me, grabbing two menus from behind the hostess stand. I wasn't one to make small talk, but I genuinely liked him.

"Fabulous as always! I assume your lovely girl Heidi will be joining you tonight?" Preston's brown eyes twinkled as he dramatically fanned himself with the menus in his hand. His thick, black hair slightly swayed from the rush of air and made me grin. It was another hot August evening and, even with the central air on, the heat from outside still managed to seep into the building. I admired that Preston was one of the oldest waiters at Happy Hour, but everyone had immediate respect for him. It was impossible to not be drawn to his friendly and caring demeanor. He reminded me of a movie star—Richard Gere with jet black hair.

Preston had a knack for overhearing conversations while feigning indifference, so he had acquired quite extensive background knowledge on our whole TPR drama from last year. One night after Heidi and I had a few too many apple martinis, Preston sat down in the booth next to us and offered some solid advice.

"Screw Topher. Your young precious lives are worth more than some dillweed who clearly has no clue what good, honest help is. You're both lucky to be rid of his sorry ass." Afterwards, he blew both of us air kisses and laughed when we gawked at him. That was when he confessed that he had overheard all our conversations, and he'd become hooked. Our lives had become a soap opera to him. He was invested. He told us we seemed like good people and—in his book—good people deserved good advice. Ever since then, Preston had become a third girlfriend to us. Eventually we opened up and found out more about his life as well. It only seemed fair, since he knew so much about us. Preston had a live-in boyfriend named Lucas. He was the *maître d'* for some hot, ritzy restaurant downtown called Lux. I read about it in the Sunday paper. I tried talking Seth into trying it while we were out one night, but he gawked at me when I showed him the online menu that conveniently left out the prices. So much for keeping the romance alive, and we weren't even married yet!

"Heidi's on her way. She texted me a few minutes ago to say she had a last-minute meeting with her boss Josie." I rolled my eyes at her name. This woman made Topher seem tame. I had heard all the horrific stories about her from Heidi, just a few months into her employment at Recruiter's Inc. This woman sounded like a straight-up nightmare, to say the least. I'm sure Heidi was more than thrilled to escape that place. I was prepared to steal a few minutes of quiet time by working on the rest of my wedding "to-do" list. It was bad enough I had Josh and Ellie's wedding in a mere few weeks, but I also had a ton left to do for my own. I asked Heidi to help me with the bulk of the tasks still left, but I felt bad making her honor that past commitment since she now had to pack up her entire life and move to another state.

Preston sat me at a booth and went to fetch two waters. I pulled out my list to see what was still unfinished.

### Two months left:
*Mail invites.* __
*Get addresses for Uncle Fletcher and Aunt Louise.* __
*Purchase wedding gifts*__
*Find makeup and hair person*__
*Final gown fitting*__
*Follow up with wedding planner*__
*Force Seth to help me with getting addresses finalized*__
*Pick cake flavor(s)*__
*Follow up with Father Mel*__

Seth wasn't very accommodating with his time when it came to assisting me with anything wedding related, but he sure enjoyed micromanaging me. He had plenty of his own opinions but didn't seem too concerned with helping me address some items on our lengthy checklist. I was more stressed by his lack of involvement than the actual tasks that needed to be done. He would ask me for an update and then make snide comments like, "Hmm, shouldn't that be done by now?" or "Babe, have you decided on what to get the wedding party yet, or how about our parents?" I was ready to release my inner bridezilla on him at any moment. Feeling defeated, I tucked the list back into my purse, depressed by my inability to check anything off it. Instead, I played around on Pinterest until Heidi arrived. I typed in *vintage style wedding cakes* and fell into a trance.

Ten minutes later I saw Heidi walking toward me with rage painted on her face. She threw her oversized, knock-off couture purse into the booth, plopped herself down across from me, and pounded the small table with her fists. *Uh-oh! This doesn't look good.*

"That wretch— Argh! I am so glad I'm leaving that hell hole!" Heidi took a sip of her water that Preston had so kindly delivered to the table before her arrival. I could only imagine this had something to do with Josie *aka* the Wicked Witch of the West.

"Uh-oh. What happened?" I had a feeling Josie put a spin on the truth once again, her typical high-school behavior. I'll bet Heidi would exchange her for Topher any day.

Preston came by at that exact moment and we placed an order for a pitcher of the house red sangria. *When in Rome* had now become *when discussing Josie;* lots of alcohol was needed. Heidi leaned forward and narrowed her dark eyes, shaking her head. I held my breath and waited for the drama to unfold.

"So, that little two-faced weasel went to HR and told them God knows what, and then they called me in right after I texted you about meeting up here. And they 'let me go.'" I watched in horror as my friend made air quotes. Heidi cackled at this, considering she had already given her notice to Josie earlier that week. With her dark eyes smoldering, she continued her rant, unfolding the rest of the story as I stared at her in shock.

"I gave them a two freaking week notice, and I had a week left to fulfill that commitment, and they just decided it wasn't necessary! Meanwhile, Josie sat in the office with me and stared me down, while Thomas—the head of HR—droned on and on about cutting ties and 'making a clean break'— whatever the hell that means. I felt completely blindsided by the whole thing! I mean, my accounts were all up-to-date, I had good rapport with my clients and my co-workers…" Heidi just kept shaking her head, attempting to figure out how this had gone south for her. She smacked the table one last time for good measure and sulked back against her chair with her arms folded.

I cleared my throat and ventured to cheer her up with a pep talk. "Maybe it was for the best. I mean, now you have more time to focus on the move and finish packing. Josie was probably just mad because everyone loved you and wished you the best. She was jealous of the attention you were receiving." Heidi tightened her arms in front of her chest and pouted for another minute, until Preston came over with our delicious-looking pitcher of alcohol. That brought a smile to her face. *Saved by the sangria!*

"You're right! Ding dong, the witch is dead," she happily chanted as she took the liberty of pouring us both full glasses of the red juice, topping both rims off with colorful pieces of fruit. I could tell Heidi was pretending to be upbeat, but I knew she was still upset. She took pride in her job and her work ethic, so being "let go" wasn't something she'd ever experienced. Sadly, I *could* relate to those feelings, considering I went through an actual termination from TPR not quite a year ago. I inwardly shivered at the mere thought, not wanting to ever relive that memory again.

I knew Heidi would drink her feelings away, so to avoid an

intoxicated and angry Heidi, I decided to humor my friend with my own horror stories of the last few weeks, hoping it would soften her own recent blow. "I'll bet I can cheer you up with more horror stories involving Ellie and her circus of a wedding." I leaned back and took a long gulp of my refreshing drink, while Heidi eagerly nodded her head to keep talking. My stories involving Ellie always amused her. I went on to tell her about the horrendous bridesmaid dress, the four-inch heels I was being forced to wear, and how my mother was loving all of this but was even more excited about becoming a first-time grandmother in three months. Every time I tried to bring up anything about my wedding, she would cut me off and gush about another cute outfit she had bought the baby. Josh and Ellie had announced they were having a baby girl, and my mother burst into tears of joy while I cried tears of ... jealousy ... annoyance ... heartache? I honestly wasn't sure, but luckily everyone else just assumed I was as happy about becoming an aunt as my mother was about becoming a grandmother. She now referred to herself as "Grammy." Heidi sat back and listened to me go on and on for a good ten minutes before she finally leaned forward and tilted her head, with a drink in one hand and a finger pointed at me from the other. *Uh-oh.* I knew that look. Heidi was preparing to step up on her soapbox.

"Bethany, I love you as a friend, and I say this out of love." A long pause cut the space between us. "You deserve to be a mother if that's what you really want. You need to marry a guy who wants and shares the same long-term visions you do. It's not fair to neglect something that huge in your life and think you are compromising for his sake. I love Seth, and I love you guys together, but, come on, do you really want to give up being a mom because he isn't sure about being a dad?" Heidi ended her speech by tossing back the rest of her sangria and reaching for the half-empty pitcher to pour herself seconds.

I sighed. After my entire spiel about the wedding and everything else, leave it to Heidi to fixate on the *baby* comments—my Achilles heel. I cleared my throat before responding. "I know you love me, but I know that Seth loves me too. He's just scared. Guys are more immature than girls, and I'm sure once he sees Baby Bowers, he will want us to have one of our own, too. It's like getting a puppy. It sounds overwhelming but, once you adopt the pup, your heart melts and you appreciate being a pet owner. At the end of the day, you know it was worth all the late nights, chewed shoes, and poop accidents." I kind of winged that last part since, lately, I'd been researching adopting dogs, hoping it could be a small step toward showing Seth how good I was at being a pet mom, so I went with it.

"Bethany, again … I love you. But you cannot compare a baby to a dog!" Heidi sounded exasperated and shook her head in disapproval as she reached for one of the menus Preston had left behind. Alcohol always made Heidi crave food. She stopped her lecture long enough to select the seafood platter, which we would both end up sharing. Then she continued where she left off. "A baby is hard work and full commitment for the rest of your life. Hell, that's why Colin and I wanted to wait a few years. We wanted to be absolutely sure this was what we both wanted. You can't exchange a baby. And you can't give up a newborn for crying all night long or having accidents. Trust me, a dog is much easier to raise!" Heidi thought she knew it all—well at least more than me—since she had grown up babysitting, nannying, and had a small stint working at a daycare. Satisfied with spewing her wisdom at me, she took a swig of her colorful drink, which was now mostly watered down with the remaining ice cubes that clinked against the glass as she set it back down on the table.

I knew Seth just needed some time. We had discussed having a baby half a dozen times over the past year. My compromise had been waiting two years after we got married to start trying, and his was a solid, five-year plan. Actually, he had the ten-plus-years plan, which all but stated, "I don't want to procreate. Let's just enjoy *us*." I had supplemented the five. His rebuttal to my much lower number was, "Let's talk about it later." That was over three months ago.

After Preston came by and took our food order and promised another (and final) pitcher of sangria, I decided to tell Heidi the half-truth. After all, white lies sometimes turned into the truth. Plus, I believed in positive affirmations. The more I repeated my short list of hopes and dreams, the more I was certain God would hear me and at least throw me a bone.

"Seth and I agreed that we would start trying for a baby two years from our wedding day." I was confident this would appease my friend, but also secretly hoped it would come true. All I had to do was show Seth we could be parents and that I was willing to do all the hard stuff, like have the baby and raise the baby, and he didn't have to do a thing. I was in my late twenties, after all. It was time to start trying before I was considered too old or, worse yet—declared barren. What if there was an issue and we couldn't conceive? Seth was a few years older than me, and I worried that the window to conceive naturally would be closing soon. I would want to know as early as possible so we could seek treatment. Heidi was in her mid-thirties. I initially thought we were around the same age and couldn't believe she was that much older than me. She and Colin were just starting to try again after suffering a loss last year, but I wanted to have a baby before turning thirty. I would be horrified to have a baby over the age of thirty-five.

Just thinking about babies made me reminisce back to the fourth grade, when I proudly told my mother and father that I was going to have two kids—first a boy (so he could protect his little sister) and then a girl—and, of course, a family dog named Oscar. I was going to marry my cute classmate, Henry

O'Doole (at the time he was my pretend boyfriend and my first school crush), and we would be married on an island in the south of France. I had developed a small obsession for traveling after my teacher, Mrs. Smyth, had introduced us to different countries and cultures in Social Studies class, and I realized the world was full of interesting people. I wanted to travel and see other countries and cities instead of staying stuck in Pittsburgh. Of course, Josh made fun of me that night, calling me a daydreamer, and squashed my dreams when earlier that day Henry stuck his tongue out at me (when I tried to hold his hand during recess—to prove Josh wrong— my first and only crucial move when it came to boys) and declared that all girls had cooties. That was the end of that dream. I was heartbroken. My parents planned a surprise trip to Greenfield, Michigan that following weekend, hoping I would forget all about my heartbreak with a little trip to the Henry Ford Museum. (I also had a small obsession with muse-ums.) I enjoyed the trip, but I never quite got over Henry, especially when he started "going out" with Kimberly Greene in the sixth grade. I always resented both of them afterwards, even though the going-out stint lasted all of three periods.


HEIDI BROUGHT me back to the present when she started talking about my semi-half true confession from a few minutes earlier. "It's a great compromise, and I'm happy you stood up for yourself."

*Little does she know how hard the battle is on this topic!* I changed the subject so I wouldn't feel too guilty about too many lies and started talking about the Kardashian wanna-be wedding that was only two weeks away. We finished our dinner and drank our second pitcher of sangria, then parted ways an hour later. I ended the night with some much-needed journaling.

· · ·

**WELCOME BACK, Bethany! Would you like to continue where you left off?**

**Great! Have fun journaling!**

I read somewhere that there is a correlation between drinking alcohol and women having a harder time conceiving. I wonder if that's why Heidi is having such a hard time getting pregnant? She does drink a lot. Look at Ellie - she doesn't drink at all, and she got knocked up right away! Maybe I should cut back on my drinking just in case that's true. I will need to drink to get myself through Josh's upcoming wedding though. And then I'll probably need to drink while I finish planning my own wedding. Alcohol has become my new BFF. Wow, that makes me sound like I have a drinking problem. No, that's nonsense. I hardly drink unless I'm out with Heidi or I've had a bad day at work, or I'm stressed about this wedding. Crap. Now that I think about it, I have been drinking every single day this past week. Not a lot, of course, but just enough to take the edge off.

Maybe Seth thinks I have a drinking problem and that's the real reason he doesn't want to have a baby with me right away! He doesn't drink much himself since both his parents are big drinkers. I guess he had some embarrassing moments growing up and didn't want to turn out the same way. How do I bring that up though? "Seth, do you think I'm codependent on alcohol—because I'm not!" Or maybe I show him instead of telling him. I think I read a book a while back called *The Five Love Languages* that teaches that everyone has a different way of showing their love to their spouse (I took the word spouse as a technicality at that time). I took the test after I bought the book on Amazon. No way was I going into a bookstore to purchase such a book! I scored needing "words of affirmation" whereas Seth was "acts of service." I know this because I made him take the test with me. Okay, technically I didn't tell him it was a test, but he complied and answered the questions.

He likes to show me his love instead of verbalizing it. Maybe I can try to show him I am not codependent on wine. Or champagne. I can make an effort of NOT drinking all week, and maybe I could give the Vitamix a whirl and make some healthy smoothies for us. We got that as an engagement gift, and it's still in the box in the basement. Maybe he'll see I am taking care of my body and it will plant the seed that I can go nine months without drinking and be perfectly fine. It must be my social drinking that has him hesitant to want a baby. It all makes sense now!

Speaking of taking care of my body... I wonder if I could nab another appointment with Vera. After seeing Ellie looking perfect in her dress, I want to make sure my dress still fits.

I instantly opened another tab on Chrome and typed "trending diets." I shuddered that I was actually thinking of dieting for a wedding dress. *Maybe my wedding should have been first.* I sighed out loud and began scanning the first page of fad diets that appeared after I hit "enter." At the same time, I was craving a triple chocolate donut from DoughNuts and immediately surrendered to the food devil perched on my left shoulder. I wandered downstairs in search of my car keys while Whole30 and Keto diet recipes flashed in the back of my mind.

# Chapter 5

It was the morning of Josh and Ellie's wedding, and it was raining. *Like they need any more luck in their lives.* If rain was a good omen for the bride and groom, it had the opposite effect on the wedding party—particularly me. I overslept by a half hour because Seth said he had set the alarm before drifting off into a snoring slumber. He didn't. Thankfully, my body clock woke me when it did.

I rushed around like a mad woman, trying to throw everything I needed into my carry-on bag, and prayed I'd make it to the hair salon on time. This was after I realized I still needed to take a shower because Ellie had asked us to come to the salon with clean and very dry hair (via a zillion texts, emails, calls, and again at the rehearsal dinner last night). In fact, she had stressed the "dry hair" part so much that I gave myself a headache before bed, from rolling my eyes every time she mentioned the word "hair." I actually made a drinking game out of it, except that I was the only one drinking. Or playing. I didn't even want to think about the perfect couple or how flawless the rehearsal was. Thankfully, I didn't have to because I had about five minutes to shower and dry my hair. It took all of my energy, but I power-dried my tresses in record time and was actually impressed with myself until I looked outside and saw it was a downpour. The universe really did hate me.

My mother had already called five times, so I started ignoring my phone. Josh had sent numerous texts asking where I was and kept mentioning that all the girls were already at the hair salon.

Instead of responding to my mother or my brother, I texted Heidi and gave her the low down on my morning thus far. I threw my cell into my carry-on and slammed the back door shut on my way to the car. I couldn't find my umbrella, so I had to run to my car, which was parked in the middle of the driveway. I had asked Seth to pull my car in for me, since he used it last to run to the store after the rehearsal dinner. His idea of pulling it all the way in meant the center of the driveway. He was really getting on my last nerve this week.

It was bad enough that I had to endure a sickeningly sweet and near-perfect rehearsal dinner at Serendipity—no joke, that was the name of the restaurant (a seafood and steak house, no less). It was a brand-new place located downtown. We had a private room, and the chef came out and personally shook hands with Josh and Ellie. How does that even happen? I'll tell you how: Josh! He apparently went to college with the chef. It was a scene right out of a Hallmark movie. So, of course, he was invited to have his rehearsal dinner there.

The entire night Seth kept commenting on how expensive everything must be and kept helping himself to glasses of wine, which was odd because I'd never seen him touch the stuff. Multiple—very expensive bottles—were given to the lucky couple, courtesy of the restaurant owner. Each retailed at about $90 a bottle. My parents gushed on and on about how delicious the food was and, at one point, my dad jokingly poked Seth in the arm and said, "No pressure, son, but let's hope Heinz Field can keep up. I wonder where their chefs are trained?" That comment turned into an hour-long conversation about classically trained chefs versus self-taught ones. I found it odd, however, that Ellie's parents were both absent. Who doesn't show up for their own daughter's rehearsal dinner? Maybe they decided to boycott this joke of a wedding!

I asked my mother when we both ended up in the restroom together, and she said that her parents' flight from Europe was delayed but they would be home bright and early in the morning. She also said her parents had paid for the entire night, including night caps for everyone. I kept waiting for my mother to comment about both parents being absent, since she is over the top when it comes to family time and values, but she didn't bat an eye. She simply smiled and commented what a beautiful night it was and summoned me to follow her back to the table. Of course, I ended up having to drive Seth and myself home since he was a little buzzed after dessert was served.

I knew I should have checked on the car myself, but an hour after we got home, Seth realized he was out of hair product and needed to run to the drug store. I offered him mine, but he refused. He was oddly obsessed with his thick, wavy hair and had this crazy nightly and morning ritual, which I gave up figuring out a long time ago. In fact, I never knew he *had* a hair routine until we moved in together. So, when he said he pulled the car all the way in last night, I stupidly believed him.

The rain, mixed with the already-muggy morning, made my fine, brown hair frizzy as I drove. I could only hope this hair stylist could handle my unmanageable mane, considering I was paying a fortune for the appointment.

The normal fifteen-minute drive to the salon turned into a half hour because of the rain. Drivers were moving like molasses. Luckily, I found parking up front and I was able to sprint to the entrance without further damage to my already-damp hair.

As I entered the busy salon, I looked around to find my party. The receptionist—a gorgeous girl with chestnut hair and flawless porcelain skin—ended her phone conversation and looked up at me. She measured the length of my body with only her bulging, hazel eyes and tapped a bright-red acrylic fingernail on her chin.

"Are you Bethany? I was just told we had one stray arrival for the Bowers' appointment." Her voice dripped with boredom, and I nodded my head to confirm that I was indeed the stray that everyone was waiting for. She pressed a button on an intercom located on her desk and notified the stylist that I had *finally* arrived. I think I saw her eyes roll as she stared me down in judgment. Anger simmered in my head. *So what if my hair is slightly wet? It's raining for heaven's sake!* I self-consciously touched a strand of my frizzy, half-dried hair and tucked it behind my ear. *This is all Seth's fault.* I imagined him still in bed, snoring logs while I faced a full-on beauty execution by a wanna-be *Sweet Valley High* former-cheerleader-turned-receptionist beauty queen! Feeling my heart quicken at the thought, I slowly breathed in and out, counting to three... *1... 2...3... Breathe.* Sometimes infomercials really are informative at 2 AM.

At that exact moment, I saw my mother briskly walking up front to greet me. I wouldn't have recognized her if it weren't for the famous scowl she carried ever so gracefully on her face. My mother preferred old-fashioned trends, such as the standard French Twist. However, this day she was modeling a perfect blowout, complete with intense makeup, clearly done by a professional. My mother pinched pennies our whole life and wasn't one to carelessly spend her money. Yet, it seemed for Josh's wedding, she had no issues shelling out the big bucks.

As my mother was about to launch into one of her be-on-time lectures, she stopped short as she took in my damp and slightly frizzy hair, most of the strands around my face already dry.

"I don't even want to know— Wait, where is your umbrella?" She tapped her hand to her forehead and then remembered she had a freshly painted face and quickly lowered her arm back down to her side. I opened my mouth to explain about Seth and the car and the missed alarm, when she cut me off with a raised hand and grabbed the sleeve of my right arm to guide me over to the other girls. "Never mind all that. I'm just glad you're here, and Arabella can fix you up. She's quite talented. Look at me!" My mother waved to the receptionist, who was back on the phone again, to let her know "the stray" had been adopted, before leading the way to the back of the salon. *Lovely. I'm getting my hair done by a girl named Arabella. Is there a stripper pole in her station, too?*

FORTY-FIVE MINUTES LATER, I had mutated into someone I didn't recognize. Since I was late on arrival, the other girls —*aka* Ellie—determined the hairstyle for everyone. Arabella, who had platinum-blond hair and piercing green eyes, promptly got busy on my tresses as soon as I made my way to her station. One glance around the room proclaimed that everyone else had already been styled, and they were now relaxing with glasses of bubbly champagne, while another girl worked on their nails one at a time. My hair was teased so high I wasn't sure if I would ever be able to shampoo it out. I looked ridiculous in a half updo, complete with Goldilocks-style curls. Arabella said the curls would eventually come loose, so she had to make them super tight; and of course, she froze them in place with a half-bottle of hairspray. My head hurt, and I wasn't sure if Seth would even recognize me. I had a suspicion that Ellie had bribed this stylist to make me look hideous. She did, after all, come from a family of money. And

—maybe for good measure—roofied then hypnotized the rest of the bridal party to say I looked fabulous. There was something definitely amiss with my mother. She never drank (it went against her religion!), yet I saw Ellie handing her a glass of champagne, which she promptly gulped down.

Once I walked over to the manicure station, Ellie and her other two bridesmaids and my mother all smiled at me and kept telling me how fabulous I looked. *Seriously, how much champagne did they drink?* I quickly sent Heidi a text, along with a selfie of my "fabulous new look," and informed her about all the attention I was receiving. Lots of sarcastic emoticons were included. When offered a glass of bubbly to drink, I downed it in two sips and immediately wanted to puke. My phone beeped and I read the text from Heidi, which came with her own set of attachments.

*OMG! You are Carrie Bradshaw in the episode "The Real Me" when she had to walk the runway and pretend she was a model. Everyone kept telling her she looked fabulous too!*

She then sent a photo of Carrie Bradshaw in her wild, runway-model outfit and hairdo. Heidi was obsessed with *Sex and the City* and would always relate anything she could to the now-syndicated show. When she wasn't watching SATC − like me − she was watching something on Bravo. TV and taste testing new wines was a hobby, wasn't it?

I quickly responded:

*What the hell do I do? I look awful … and this is real life! I can't look like this for my brother's wedding. I'm a freak!*

I was next to get my nails done, so I was running out of time to keep texting my only sane lifeline.

Another beep.

*Just keep it together and pretend for their sake. We'll fix it once you get home. I'll come over and make you look normal again. I gotta go. Remember, just smile and be nice. I'll see you in an hour. Oh, and make sure we have wine.*

*Be nice? Easier said than done.*

Thank God for Heidi. The thought of losing her to another state instantly made me feel weepy again, and I had to blink back tears. This was going to be a very long day. I reached for another glass of champagne, and this time I sipped it slowly.

## Chapter 6

Seth was already gone by the time I pulled into our driveway. Josh had requested all the groomsmen meet at his apartment for pre-ceremony drinks. Probably for the best, considering I didn't even recognize myself in the mirror after my horrendous makeover. My head hurt from all the champagne I had drunk at the salon to calm my nerves. I reached in my purse to pop an Advil. God was punishing me. I pounded my head on my steering wheel as I sat in the middle of my driveway, having a mini meltdown.

The wedding started at four, and it would all take place at the venue, not a church. Although Father Mel wasn't part of the ceremony, my mother had made sure he was on the guest list. One of Josh's buddies from college agreed to be the officiant for the wedding and had apparently gotten certified a few years back. I would have died of embarrassment, and I thought my parents would too, but apparently my mother took this news without a major meltdown. I was shocked. In fact, everything about my parents' reactions to my brother's wedding shocked me. I later discovered that Josh sat down with my parents awhile back and told them that Ellie wasn't affiliated with a church, and it would be uncomfortable for her to get married in one. The truth was that Ellie and her family were agnostic and didn't believe in God. Of course, Josh would never come out and say that, so he, once again, made his baby momma look sweet and innocent. Who doesn't believe in God? My parents, being gullible, embraced his story and didn't ask too many questions. *Seriously? Their future daughter-in-law is anti-Christmas and those two—die-hard Catholics—were okay with this?*

Could no one but me see right through this girl? She was only after Josh for his money. And today she would be sealing the deal and getting the perfect wedding every girl dreams about.

Apparently, the fact that I was getting married in a Catholic church was sufficient for them, and they were okay with letting Josh "do his own thing." How nice, considering Seth and I had originally wanted to have our wedding and reception on site at the venue as well, but my father quickly put his foot down about having Father Mel marry us, once my mother became visibly upset with our plan last Christmas Eve. The fact that they were helping us pay for our wedding also meant abiding by some of their rules and requests.

Thank God Heidi was coming over to salvage some of this day. Hopefully, I could get back on track afterwards. She had texted me to wash my hair as soon as I got home so she could start working on me the moment she arrived. I did what I was told and welcomed the hot water crashing down on my beat-up body. It took three washes before my hair felt soft again and not like dried-up bubble gum on an old leather shoe. Ugh. I was going to write a horrible Yelp review to warn anyone who respected their hair to steer clear of Arabella!

Twenty minutes later—after my glorious shower and feeling confident I had my real hair back—I had gotten rid of my headache and was scrubbing my face when my phone went off. I splashed one last round of warm water on my forehead before patting it dry and checking my screen. It was

Seth. His text made no sense. I tried to read it twice. This wasn't good. Seth rarely drank. God, I was going to strangle my brother—wedding or not!

*Babe - Let's get a dog! Josh is in love with being a dad and I fink I can be a fur dad. We don't need kids if we have pets. We could be fur parents! Oh, and let's buy a fireball at the grocery store next week. It's good!*

Then there was a short line of dog emojis and random letters ending his convo.

Fireball? Seth was drinking Fireball? Oh, for the love of—I was definitely going to murder Josh now. Seth could barely handle the light stuff, like a few beers or the three glasses of wine he downed the other night (he complained about a stomachache for the rest of the night). Now he was drinking Fireball? This is the same guy who once got drunk off two Christmas Ales on New Year's Eve and passed out before the ball dropped, leaving me to ring in the New Year by myself.

I balled my fists up and willed myself to take a deep breath. *No, Seth! A dog will NOT replace a baby.* Why did he not want to have a child with me? I thought that by now I would have changed his mind about parenting. Now his big plan was to buy a dog—a puppy, no less—and he thought I would be satisfied with this? And to top it off, he was drunk! I felt the tears forming behind my very tired eyes, and I willed myself not to cry. *I'm such an idiot for bringing up being a dog owner and thinking that would change anything in the long run.*

"Pull it together, Bowers!" I chastised myself as I threw more water on my face to hide the red blotches that had started to form across my cheeks. I couldn't lose it now. I had to hold it together for my brother's ridiculous wedding and surround myself with family and friends in mere hours. I took a few more deep breaths and then sent Heidi a text that the door would be open, and I would be upstairs drying my hair.

. . .

THIRTY MINUTES later Heidi and I were bonding over a bottle of Pinot Noir as she finished curling the last piece of my hair. I had managed to hold it together and, after drying my hair, I happily played hostess by cutting up some cheese and hard salami and throwing some crackers on a plate, which I presented as an offering, while Heidi uncorked the wine.

Heidi helped herself to another delicate meat-and-cheese sandwich as I filled her wine glass, thankful for her company. As much as I wanted to tell her about Seth's awful drunk text message, I couldn't bring myself to do it. Plus, I didn't think I could go through another round of tears, especially when I knew she would tell me, "I told you so." So, we chatted about other things while she worked her magic.

A few minutes later, Heidi stood back and acknowledged her masterpiece, and I inwardly cringed as I watched her give me the once over. I truly trusted my friend, but after the day I'd had, I could only imagine the worst. I held my breath as she tucked a stray piece of hair behind my ear then finished by covering my head with her *extra hold* hairspray. I felt the stickiness land on my bare arms, and I finally gave in.

"Let me see…" I opened my eyes and then made my way to the mirror, which hung over our tiny bathroom sink. I looked like myself again, only prettier! I couldn't believe it. Heidi had managed to recreate the same style Ellie requested, only this time I now looked presentable enough to show my face in public. Soft, flowing curls were held back with bobby pins that blended into my dark hair, and simple yet gorgeous crystal-studded pins were masterfully woven through the top strands.

"Are you sure Arabella even has a *real* cosmetology license?" Heidi laughed as she took another swig of her red wine. I knew she was impressed with her work, and I secretly felt a bout of jealousy for a brief moment. *I wish I had a talent like that.* My only talent seemed to be recapping the latest episode of The Real Housewives or Top Chef.

"I wouldn't believe it after her hack job on my hair this morning. You should have seen everyone, Heidi. They were all oohing and ahhing like she did some amazing transformation or something. I looked like a freak! I think they were all hammered on cheap champagne." I shuddered at the earlier memory before taking a sip of my own wine and making a mental note to never ever drink champagne again.

"Well, you now look presentable, thanks to your *amaaazing* friend of many talents." Heidi smirked and gave me a quick hug. Something was definitely off with her, but I couldn't put my finger on it. Not to mention, I was still trying to sort out my own internal drama.

"Thank you. I owe you so much." I reached out and gave her another half hug, careful not to touch my hair. I knew I was cutting it close on time and I needed to finish getting ready to meet everyone at the venue. I was dreading putting my dress on, but I had no choice. *It's one night. I can do this for Josh.* Besides, I would find a way to make him repay me.

"I'm going to pack up my stuff and run to the bathroom. I'll meet you downstairs. Okay?" Heidi started to reach for her accessories, and I offered to help her clean up.

"Girl, you need to finish getting ready. I've got this." She shooed me out of the bathroom. I had to agree with her. I really needed to finish getting ready.

Ten minutes later I heard Heidi knock on my bedroom door without coming in. I was halfway dressed and trying to get the resistant zipper up on the back of my horrific dress. I pinched myself a few times, in hopes that I was indeed dreaming. Fat chance. This was no nightmare. It was my life, but at least I was continuing this nightmare with good hair.

"Come in!" I yelled through the door. *Why can't I get this zipper up?*

"I'm taking off. You look great! I hope you can *try* to enjoy your night." I heard Heidi's muffled voice through the door.

*Noooo! She didn't hear me, and I need her help with this zipper!*

"Wait! Come back! I can't—" I tried to run to the door, but I tripped over the feathers at the bottom of my dress and nearly fell to the floor, barely catching myself at the last minute.

By the time I opened the door, she was gone. Poof! My fairy godmother had disappeared.

In one last effort, I tugged as hard as I could at the stubborn zipper and heard a ripping sound.

*You have got to be kidding me!*

# Chapter 7

I stood in awe of the massive building in front of me, waiting to be picked up and devoured by its overwhelming size any minute. It was a monstrosity! I knew the William Penn Hotel was fancy, but that statement was underrated in comparison to seeing it in person. *John F Kennedy stayed in this hotel, and now my brother is getting married here!* My heart was beating fast and hard at this comparison. My mouth fell open at some point, until my uncharacteristically giddy mother nudged me and grabbed my arm to pull me forward. "Bethany, isn't this just gorgeous?" she gushed. "I can't believe Ellie was able to book their wedding here. Everyone is going to be thrilled. I'll bet the food is amazing. After all, it *better* be, considering how much they probably paid for everything, not that it's any of my business. Your father and I had a very modest wedding compared to what you kids do these days." My mother made her usual tsk-tsk sounds when it came to money and material-istic expenses, but she quickly redeemed herself when she saw a few early guests making their way up the inviting path that led to the entrance of the grand hotel. She waved and briskly walked over to greet them, leaving my father and me standing in awkward silence on the sidewalk. My father chuckled then winked at me and said, "I raised smarty-pants kids, all right. You kids did good for yourselves. Your mother and I are proud of you and your brother." He cleared his throat, mildly embarrassed for showing his emotion, and the two of us— followed by my mother, who had now walked back towards us —made our way to the main doors of the William Penn Hotel. For someone who scolded over the "extravagance of one day," she sure was eating this up.

*If I can make it through the next six or so hours without any further mishap, it will be a miracle.* I'd had to call my mother for help after I ripped the zipper on the back of my bridesmaid dress. I was mortified that I had ruined the dress and would then somehow ruin my brother's wedding in the process. As much as I didn't care for Ellie, I loved my brother, and even though it was a love-hate relationship at times, I wanted this day to be everything he dreamed of. Thankfully, my mother was a genius when it came to sewing, and she was able to fix the zipper in record time. Of course, I got an ear full of how irresponsible I was - like it was my fault the zipper decided to malfunction! I was then subjected to riding with my parents to the ceremony, still cringing and hoping that Seth had sobered up by now. After the zipper issue, I decided to text Seth back, but he never responded. Before I could become angry and react, my parents had shown up and I didn't have time to worry about it. Now I was just hoping I could get through the ceremony without tripping over my dress—or worse yet— having the patched zipper come loose and showcase my very worn strapless bra and granny panties for all the guests to stare at in mock horror, mid-ceremony! The thought made me involuntarily reach behind my dress to feel for the patched-up zipper, which was ever-so-slightly poking me in the back.

MY EYES BULGED and I had to catch my breath as the three of us walked through the main doors and into the lavish lobby.

*Okay, Josh wins!* Compared to this place, our wedding was going to look like child's play, even though Heinz Field was nothing to be ashamed about. It wasn't enough that Josh lived in a luxury apartment overlooking downtown. And it wasn't enough that he had a good job at an engineering firm. Now he had to one-up me even further and have a better wedding. *And the first grandchild!*

I had a few minutes before I needed to make my way to the bridal suite, so I tried to inconspicuously take a few photos with my cell phone. Some of the hotel attendants walked by and smiled when they saw me all decked out in my gaudy, white, mermaid-style tulle dress, complete with an ungodly amount of bird feathers trailing at the ends. I plastered a tight smile to my face and acted like this type of dress was normal to wear to a wedding. *At least my hair looks good.* I wanted to defend myself and tell these strangers that this wedding was a hoax. After all, it was based on Kim Kardashian's first wedding and Ellie was determined to replicate *everything* Kim did. At the moment I was wearing my comfortable slip-on shoes. I refused to wear those horrendous four-inch high-heeled rhinestone shoes that Ellie had graciously purchased on my behalf. Unfortunately, those were currently dangling from my right hand, due to my mother's sudden recollection as we were leaving the house. "Bethany, don't forget those gorgeous shoes now," she cooed as we all rushed out the door. Who was this woman?! I was never allowed to even wear half-inch heels as a teenager, and now she was encouraging me to wear stripper shoes?

The lobby certainly didn't disappoint. Large crystal chandeliers hung from the enormous ceiling, and shades of goldish-orange jabot drapes adorned the tall, oval-shaped windows that lined the perimeter of the whole lobby. The whole ensemble was very reminiscent of the Neoclassical era with the classic columns creating the oval architecture to give the room an old-world-charm feel. Off to the side was a baby grand piano, and I wondered if it was just a display or if they actually hired someone to sit and play beautiful ballots while guests walked through. Small wingback chairs were scattered throughout to create an inviting atmosphere. In fact, all that was missing was a roaring fireplace and a butler. This hotel reeked of money—something my brother also had over me.

As I stood lost in thought, my mother startled me from behind. "Bethany—we need to get you to the bridal suite. Oh gosh, I can't wait to see what *that* looks like. I can't believe Joshua is getting married and giving me a grandbaby all in the same year!" Clapping her hands, my mother was no longer talking to me as her eyes glazed over at the mention of the baby, and her hand flew to her chest to make the sign of the cross. Now I was back to being annoyed, and I snapped at her. "Mom, what are you doing? Wait—are you really praying?" I looked at her in disbelief and noticed she had pulled her good strand of rosary beads out from God knows where and now had them entangled in her hands. My mother defended her actions as if it were a personal attack on God himself and she snapped back, "There is nothing wrong with praying, young lady! I am talking to the Lord to make sure all goes well tonight, and in a few months for my first grandbaby." My mother whispered one more prayer then placed her rosary beads back in her small, sparkling gold clutch, which matched her shimmery beige dress. I did a double take at her purse, which I just noticed she was holding, and sputtered out incoherently, "Where—how did...Wait—you bought a Kate Spade bag?" I stopped moving, which made my mother almost walk into me from behind.

"Oh… Ellie bought me this as a gift when we went shopping and picked out this dress." My mother waved the small clutch in front of me "She's just so sweet and generous." I rolled my eyes and tried to suppress the sigh that was threatening to escape my throat. *Sweet? Generous?* I was beginning to think my whole family had fallen prey to this girl. *Everyone but me.* Maybe it was time I spoke my mind and told Ellie—or better yet—w*arn* her she'd better be marrying my brother for love. But first I needed lots of liquid courage, so I was hoping there was some champagne in this bridal suite. Ellie herself was a teetotaler, but Josh talked her into having alcohol for the wedding—for him. *Bless you, Josh!*

THE BRIDAL SUITE was on the fifth floor, which could have been mistaken for the penthouse suite because it was so big. *Seriously, how in the world can Josh afford this? Ellie doesn't even work!* I felt the anger creeping up my face and swiped a full glass of alcohol, which was thankfully set up near the foyer as soon as we walked through the door. I didn't even care if my mother launched into her abstinence speech. I needed a drink before I exploded. Sadly, my mother didn't even acknowledge me once we walked into the room, as she was immediately drawn to Ellie, who was sitting fully dressed and getting the final touches of her hair and makeup done in the center of the room. You would have thought Ellie was her long-lost daughter from overseas as she ran to her and shrieked (as best my mother knew how) and gently kissed both of her cheeks. Ellie looked radiant in her Vera Wang white ball gown. Her hair was done up in a gorgeous ballerina bun, which was offset by a crystal-encrusted headband. And damn her, she still didn't even look six months pregnant! Her dress had a sweet-heart neckline, dusted in fine crystals, and delicate tulle glided from her waist down to the floor. It was perfect.

A beautiful, tall and toned, older blonde woman with the same crisp blue eyes Ellie inherited, came forth and embraced my mother in a stiff half hug. "You must be Marybeth. I'm Ellie's mum Portia. It's a pleasure to finally meet you." She spoke in a European accent, which only made her more appealing. My mother took this woman in, and I could feel her swoon, like she had just met someone famous. "Oh, it's so wonderful to finally meet *you*, Portia. I can't wait for you to meet my husband Anthony." My mother stared up in awe at the other woman, who could literally double as Barbie's twin. Ellie's mom was drop-dead gorgeous and probably dabbled in modeling at one point in her life. She looked like she had traveled the world and was just dropping by to witness her daughter's wedding before fleeing the country again. Josh had never mentioned her parents before, so I had no idea what they did for a living other than travel for sport. I would be shocked if he even knew. Portia nodded politely but seemed a bit stand-offish, and I wondered how she felt about her only daughter being pregnant, and if she was in favor of this marriage at all. I was about to introduce myself when Portia's cell rang and she quickly answered it, briskly fleeing into the hallway, the door loudly closing behind her. I saw Ellie flinch as a quick wave of sadness washed over her but was quickly replaced by a radiating white smile as she redirected her focus to those still in the room.

Ellie made her way over to us and embraced my mother, squealing in delight. "Oh, Marybeth, you look gorgeous." She held my mother in front of her, and I noticed my mom's face flush and her eyes glisten with tears. *Oh brother.* I caught myself rolling my eyes. My mother fully embraced her back and cried, "Oh nonsense, you are the gorgeous one - and please call me Mom! None of this Marybeth formal stuff. You're family now. Right, Bethany?" My mother continued to beam, and Ellie squeezed her hand then abruptly hugged me as she squealed to the rest of the wedding party in the room, "Everyone, meet my new mom and sister!" This time I didn't hold back on my eye roll as everyone else cheered.

THIRTY MINUTES later the ceremony started, and I let myself get misty-eyed when Josh read his own vows. I looked up at Seth—one of the three groomsmen—and he had a goofy look on his face, fidgeting like a five-year-old. I noticed the other two groomsmen were standing up straight on either side of him and paying attention to the officiant. One of Josh's friends turned and whispered something into Seth's ear, and he quickly nodded back, causing the other groomsmen to nod their heads in understanding. *What the heck is wrong with him?*

I was hoping no one else would notice my fiancé's bizarre behavior. Thankfully, the ceremony was over and everyone paired up to walk out of the room while cheers and shouts exploded for the happy couple. Seth grabbed my arm and was pulling me down the makeshift aisle so fast I almost tripped over my dress, which seemed to be a theme today.

"What in the world is wrong with you?" I gritted my teeth, trying to keep my voice down, while praying no one was witnessing this embarrassing interaction.

Seth continued to briskly walk down the aisle until we exited the room, and then he finally turned to me.

"I have to piss, like really bad. I think my bladder might explode. Probably shouldn't have drunk that last beer." With a lopsided smile, he gave me a quick peck on the cheek and ran toward the bathroom leaving me standing alone, yet surrounded by a room full of cheerful, smiling wedding guests. This was my husband-to-be. Lucky me.

## Chapter 8

Cocktail hour was just beginning, and we were all ushered into the Grand Ballroom of the hotel. I made my way into the impressive 6,000-square-foot room, which included a two-tier ballroom, with dramatic balconies scattered throughout. All I could do was stare at the breathtaking baccarat crystal chandeliers and ornate gold-leaf railings, which brought the room to life. There were posh waiters scattered throughout holding trays of piping-hot food and sparkling-white drinks in crisp black uniforms. The walls dared me to walk forward and, for a moment, I forgot where I was and slowly let the feeling move me toward the center of the room.

I took in a deep breath and closed my eyes as I slowly exhaled and wondered what it would be like to be surrounded by this level of beauty every day. As I went to take another step forward, the heel of my shoe slid on the newly waxed floors and I felt my balance shift, sending me tumbling to the floor. I tried to brace myself but ended up stepping on the bottom portion of my dress, which housed enough feathers to qualify me as an endangered bird. As I lay there, face down on the cool, slick surface, all I could think was, *I am burning this horrid dress in the morning!*

I rose to my feet and straightened my back, praying no one had noticed my fumble. No such luck. A young waiter sprinted toward me with an outstretched hand in my face.

"Ouch. That looked rough." He laughed as he balanced me with both his hands on either side of my shoulders.

"You okay, Miss?" He had a genuine smile and inviting eyes the color of mocha, with just a few freckles scattered across his face—giving him an innocent presence. He looked young. *Very* young. But, very hot! Top Gun's Tom Cruise kind of hot. *Wait— did he just call me Miss?*

I cleared my throat and waved his question away with my hand, failing miserably at hiding my humiliation. "Yes, thank you. The floors are slippery." I gave a tight smile as my eyes searched the room for a glass of champagne nearby. *So much for giving up the bubbly.*

"I'm Cole, and I think those shoes are a little to blame. How do you women walk in those things? Is there a mandatory class to take before being allowed to purchase something that high?" His eyes were glued to my shoes, but his voice held laughter. *Was he mocking me?*

I cursed Ellie in my head for making me wear these death traps against my will, as this gorgeous guy stared my feet down, trying to hide a laugh.

"I'm Bethany…" I grimaced and then added, "The *bride* is trying to secretly kill me, I think. She bought these shoes for me as a bridal gift." Angry butterflies took flight in my stomach the longer I thought about it, and then I remembered I had been looking for my still-slightly drunk fiancé before I did the faceplant. He was still nowhere to be found.

"Well, keep an eye on the bride. I'd hate to see what she buys for people she *doesn't* like." Cole winked at me and started to walk away. I smiled as I watched his lean, sculpted frame move a few steps away. *What is it about this guy that I can't take my eyes off him?* As if sensing someone staring at him, he turned around and smiled at me, pointing to the far end of the room.

"Come see me for a drink later if you'd like. I'm bartending on the south side of the room. Just be careful walking over." With that, he winked at me and headed for his station.

"BETHANY!" A familiar voice shouted my name and I turned to see Seth headed toward me with a plate of food piled high in one hand and a pilsner glass filled with a dark brown liquid in the other.

*Unbelievable! He is still drinking?* I could just see the look on my mother's face and the lecture I would receive later about how I needed to keep an eye on Seth's *"drinking problem."* That was all I needed.

"This place is fancy-schmancy." Seth whistled loudly and tasted some sort of brown, stuffed strudel by inching the appetizer plate close to his mouth and using his teeth to cut it in half, since his hands remained full.

"What are you doing? Sit down and eat like a human being. We are at the William Penn Hotel!" I sneered through my teeth and willed myself not to smack my still-half-drunk fiancé. *Please let me get through dinner without incident.* The way this night was going, I could easily see myself choking on my food, Seth being oblivious and no one else even noticing while I slowly died on one of their gold Chiavari chairs. I would slither down to the cold, marble floor like a dead snake and go unnoticed until someone's foot smacked against my cold body. I shivered at the thought and tried to refocus on something more positive—like the cute waiter.

I looked around to see if Cole would be witnessing my second humiliating moment of the night, but I didn't see him. Plus, the room was so big I figured he was flooded with cocktail requests from the budding lines forming around all ends of the ballroom. I saw my parents sitting down at their table, deep in conversation with another couple. I could only imagine what they were talking about. My eyes surveyed the rest of the ballroom, but thankfully no one seemed to be paying any attention to us. Seth's dark suit was already starting to wrinkle, and his tie was already loosened around his neck. How could he be in shambles in this short of a time frame? I inhaled deeply and slowly let the air out in one long puff, deflating my cheeks and quite possibly my spirit.

Seth obeyed my demands and sat down on the closest chair and began inhaling the rest of his food. "Eh—I think we need to make our way to the head table soon. Let me just scarf this down, then we can load up again. There's some good stuff being passed around." Seth was half talking to himself, and I was half listening. A waitress carrying a large tray of champagne weaved her way by us, and I flagged her down. As I selected a tall glass of expensive bubbly, I asked her what type of food they were passing around. My stomach was rolling with hunger.

"What are those weird-looking hors d'oeuvres I've seen floating by tonight?"

"The bride is vegan, so no meat; but, if you need a little protein, there is a mushroom table near the entrance. The Chef had a blast creating this menu." The server beamed at me as she gushed about the great food being presented tonight.

I gave her a look that screamed: *Are you serious? My options are raw or cooked vegetables? Have carbs been blacklisted by the teetotaler too?*" Oblivious to my inward outrage, she continued without missing a beat, "Anyway, great party, isn't it? Have fun tonight." She smiled and continued to weave her way through the tables that were slowly filling up. I looked over at Seth, who was licking his fingers in between sips of beer. *Such a caveman.*

I peered over at the mushroom table. *I am in hell.*

# Chapter 9

**Welcome back, Bethany! Would you like to continue where you left off?**
   **Great! Have fun journaling!**
   I sat there staring at the screen for a few minutes. Maybe it was time I sought professional help. I should've been excited and happy planning my wedding and looking forward to becoming a wife, but lately all I could do was find doubt in my decision. It didn't help that I randomly met Cole at my brother's wedding. Why was I thinking about another guy? I should have been thinking about Seth. Every time I pictured Seth I felt a scowl form on my face, then I immediately felt guilt flood my insides. *What is wrong with me? Who gets annoyed thinking about their flipping fiancé?!* I inhaled a deep breath and ignored the tears forming behind my eyes. I tried to think of the last time I felt those butterflies in my stomach when I imagined Seth, but my mind went blank. I blinked a few times. *This can't be right.* There had to be a recent memory where I felt those little love bubbles floating all around me. There was that time a few months ago where he pulled my chair out for me when we went out to eat. But I realized he was about to sit down himself, and I bumped into him as I went to bend into the

chair. Or that time where he let me pick out a movie for date night. Of course, he ended up falling asleep twenty minutes into *Failure to Launch*. I scrunched my eyebrows remembering that night. I was so annoyed thinking he was actually going to give one of my favorite movies (and actors!) a chance until he started snoring like a freight train next to me, with his hand still in the popcorn bowl.

*Maybe if I chant his name, I can awaken the wedding goddess (that must be a real thing, right?) and remove this curse on myself, or at least straighten myself out.*

"Seth! Seth! Seth!"

I didn't feel anything. *Maybe it's a slow process.* I figured wedding goddesses were probably in high demand, and I was sure to be at the end of the line.

*Okay, every time I even think about Cole, I'm going to pinch myself!* Surely physical pain will reverse the curse. *"Oh my god, I'll bet Ellie cursed me! Or maybe she hired Cole and is trying to set me up to ruin my marriage!"*

"You're losing it, Bethany. Get a grip! There is no wedding goddess!"

I had to keep my hands busy to calm my mind, so I finally started typing....

I can't believe I actually just pinched myself, numerous times, and hard! Why am I thinking about Cole so much? I keep telling myself it's just nerves. I'll bet if I were to log onto one of the bridal chatrooms, I would see many posts from nervous brides like myself. I'm getting into my own head. Seth loves me, and I love him. I'm going to get married and have a wonderful life. I can get him to come around to starting a family. I'm sure it's just his nerves causing him to freak out about the kids thing. Guys do that sometimes.

My cell rang and I saw Heidi's name flash across my screen. I logged out of the website and swiped my finger to the right of my phone and greeted her. "Hey there. How's the packing going?" I tried to sound chipper as I poured myself a second glass of red and grabbed a block of cheese from the fridge. I was starving and realized I hadn't eaten all day. *So much for my "no drinking" policy. So far all I've managed to do is drink!*

I heard Heidi moan on the other end of the line and let her go off on a tangent about the movers they hired and how she still had half a townhouse to pack up. Colin wanted to start packing and moving as much as they could, and spend each weekend driving back and forth between both cities so they just had the big furniture to haul the following month.

"Well, I would have called you sooner, but I had to play caretaker to Seth because he was nursing a massive hangover the next day, and somehow it was *my* problem, too." I launched into the wedding nightmare, carefully leaving out how I fell on my face and how cute the bartender was who rescued me.

"Okay, but tell me the truth…was the hotel as amazing as it looks in pictures?" Heidi was obsessed with the William Penn Hotel, and I promised her a detailed description of each square foot of the entire venue. If I closed my eyes, I could still see and feel the ambiance of the whole ballroom and, of course, Cole and his adorable boyish grin. *Stop it, Bethany! An engaged woman should not be thinking about another man!* What was wrong with me?

"It was damn near perfect. No—it *was* perfect. Josh outdid me once again, and now my own wedding is going to look like child's play." I sounded terser than I meant to. I wondered why I was being so emotional but chalked it up to wedding stress.

I pictured Heidi rolling her eyes through the phone. "Oh please, Bethany. You're going to have an amazing wedding. Heinz Field is gorgeous and amazing in its own way. You can't compare yourself to your brother. Besides, I'm sure Ellie and her family had a say in the venue. She seems to come from old money, and I'll bet her parents pushed for something elaborate."

I cleared my throat. "Oh yeah, that reminds me. I met Ellie's mom, excuse me— "mum." She is gorgeous. It's like that whole family gets airbrushed when they wake up every morning. I've deemed them the 'plastic' family." Ellie's parents were the real-life version of Ken and Barbie—dreamhouse and all! I imagined they each had their own Porsche or Mercedes along with a personal driver that knew all about their personal lives and probably had to sign umpteen NDA forms before being hired. They didn't seem like people who drove themselves.

I went on to describe the ceremony and their perfect reception that went off without a hitch. Ellie's maid of honor gave a heartfelt speech and even I had tears in my eyes when she was done. Josh's best man also gave a speech, except he was funny and had everyone in tears from *laughing*. My brother and Ellie literally had the most perfect wedding, down to their flawless speeches! Weddings always made me weepy, but I was annoyed when I looked over to see Seth on his phone hardly paying attention during the speeches. I also opted to leave that detail out of the conversation with Heidi. When I ended my story with the ridiculous mushroom table, I nearly choked on the last sip of my wine when I heard screaming through the phone. "What the hell is a mushroom table?" I laughed out loud. Leave it to Heidi to state the obvious!

I giggled back. "Exactly what I said! Apparently, I was the only one who thought it was bizarre. Of course, Seth was eating everything in sight, like usual. He doesn't even like mushrooms! Then again, he was hammered, and I had to keep him away from my parents all night to avoid the riot act about marrying *an alcoholic*."

Heidi gasped. "Seth was hammered? No way!" She knew that Seth rarely drank, so I guess it would be shocking to hear that he was the one who got drunk, and not me for once. I cringed knowing I'd just embarrassed Seth in the future because the next time Heidi saw him, she would definitely tease him about this incident. I tried to backpedal and act like it wasn't that big of a deal.

"Well, you know my parents. One drink is an issue in their minds." At least that part was true. I still had to hide my liquor when my parents decided to drop by and visit. At this point, they knew I drank but still frowned upon it, and it was easier to just avoid their disappointing looks and curb the abstinence speech altogether.

Heidi took the bait and agreed about my parents and their stance on alcohol. We talked for a few more minutes before she let me go to finish packing yet another room. The thought of Heidi leaving the state and putting a strain on our close friendship made me sad. She was one of my closest friends and I feared that once she moved to Cleveland, our friendship would never fully get unpacked.

## Chapter 10

The following week flew by, and I was grateful to get back to my normal routine, even if it was somewhat mundane. Seth bounced out of bed Monday morning and acted like nothing had happened and his drunken behavior at the wedding was of no consequence. Maybe people who were accustomed to drinking would just chalk it up to another wedding hangover and fuzzy memories of the night before. Seth, however, seldom drank and therefore couldn't determine his cut-off limit, and then spent all of Sunday in bed moaning, complaining, or sleeping. I was mad at him because we had made plans to work on our own wedding to-do list and, once again, I was stuck dealing with it.

What really irked me the most was that last year Seth had hired a wedding planner to ease the load off my back, but she ended up being a flake and stopped responding to my emails and phone calls a few months ago. I had no idea where Seth found her. He swears she had a legit business, but I always thought something seemed off with her. Her name was Tina Hansen, and she was supposed to be my VIP—Very Important Planner—for our wedding day. She now had the title "Very *Invisible* Planner" instead. Since I had been unemployed

for a while after TPR, I was able to do most of the prepara-
tions myself, and to eliminate much of the cost, we asked her
to provide her services for the day-of only.

I should have listened to my gut after our initial meeting.
You could tell that Tina had always been a bridesmaid, never
a bride. She was middle-aged and self-admittedly never
married. She wore a dreamy expression on her face when I
told her how Seth and I met. Also, the dress she wore that day
was a recycled bridesmaid dress that was a good twenty years
out of fashion. I cringed when I saw the exact same dress in
her wedding portfolio that she provided to clients for past
services. She had used examples of her best friend's wedding
that she was in and was wearing the same dress in the photo. I
don't think she even realized it.

I remember voicing my concerns to Seth later that night,
but he shrugged it off and said he already gave her a deposit,
so we had to keep her. I believe his exact words were, "Maybe
she's frugal and didn't want to throw away a perfectly good
dress. I think it's creative of her to recycle an article of
clothing that held so much meaning to her." I can recall
rolling my eyes and thinking, *Ya, kinda like you with your inability
to throw anything away, even past the point of holes and tears.* The real-
life term for that was Cheap.

So, by Wednesday, I welcomed the longer hours that
Embeth had approved at the museum. She knew I was saving
every penny possible for our upcoming wedding and agreed to
give me a few more days on the payroll than I was originally
hired for. I was working an open-to-close shift and felt a bit of
wicked satisfaction knowing Seth would have to fend for
himself for the evening. I spoiled that man by always prepping
and cooking dinner and then cleaning up every night, by
myself. He had the audacity to ask what I was making him
Tuesday night, since I wouldn't be home to cook us dinner the
following evening.

Lately I felt he was taking my generosity for granted. Of

course, I liked to cook and enjoyed making his favorite dishes, but it would be nice if he would occasionally offer to lend a hand or even learn how to cook something simple. The man couldn't even make a decent grilled cheese sandwich! Who can't cook two buttered slices of bread held together by cheese? I immediately feel bad and recognize that his mother was the queen of frozen dinners, so he probably never learned how to make good food growing up. The thought stirs a sour feeling in my stomach and I inadvertently think about all the frozen dinners she has served over the last few holidays. Seriously, who defrosts a frozen cake for Christmas? I don't mean a homemade-save-for-a-special-occasion cake. I mean a store-bought frozen one with no thought behind it. It was nice to open the museum and have the entire building to myself for a few hours before the other employees drifted through the door. I knew Embeth would be out all day. She had some spa day planned with her girlfriends. I only knew this because I had to look at her day planner earlier this week while speaking to an interested buyer about a private showing. Some days I fantasized about what it would feel like to be Embeth for a day. She was full of power and wealth, and sometimes I wished I had that kind of life.

Then again, I couldn't imagine what it would be like to go through a divorce—a high-profile one, no less. I still couldn't understand after all this time, and everything she went through, why she would keep his last name. Whatever her reasoning, she carried that last name like she owned it.

After disarming the alarms and doing a quick walk-through of the museum, I made a pot of coffee. I carried my mug into the main foyer and walked behind the small-but-pristine desk that housed one computer, a phone, and our assignments for the week. Two chairs were also set up and consumed the area when both seats were occupied. I immediately frowned, knowing that Kendall was working the mid-day shift. I wasn't in the mood to hear about her drama.

I sipped on my hot coffee and replayed the conversation I'd had with Cole from Saturday night over and over in my head. He was so easy to talk to, and I immediately sensed a familiarity about him even though I had never met him before that night. His soft caramel eyes were so inviting. I felt as if I could trust him with my deepest secrets.

*I've never felt this way about another guy before. Am I cheating on Seth?* My mind raced a mile a minute and guilt flooded my head as I tried to push thoughts of another man out of my vision. *It's just wedding jitters. It's normal to feel anxious. I am going to devote myself to one man for the rest of my life. This is a big deal!* I pinched myself out of guilt, even though I knew it wouldn't work. I sighed and tried to picture Seth in his tux, waiting for me at the altar. The thought made me smile. Seth and I were a good match. We belonged together. I had invested time and energy into this relationship, and it would be stupid for me to throw that all away over a simple case of nerves. Plus, dating was on my Top 5 Worst Fears list - it came before dying. Dating is not for the weak of heart, and I am weak. I never would have met Seth if it weren't for my terrible telemarketing job that my parents' neighbor basically handed me at a low point in my life.

My fingers tapped out a rhythm on the marble makeshift desk, and I admired my vintage engagement ring, which seemed to flash a message that said, *"Remember me?"* as it sparkled on my left finger.

I knew Seth loved me, and we could work our differences out down the line, but I also wondered if Cole wanted to become a father and have a family of his own someday. *Why am I even thinking crazy things like this – about another man?!* At that exact moment, the main door chimed and I looked up to see a familiar face smiling at me.

"Hi, Bethany. What a surprise to see you here!" His smooth voice was just as I remembered it from the other night. My knees went weak behind the desk. Was I dreaming this? I blinked twice for extra measure, but he was still standing in front of me.

"Cole, what are you doing here?"

# Chapter 11

I stared back at Cole while trying to pick my jaw up from the floor. *Oh great! I managed to pick up a stalker. Leave it to me to do that!* Of course, I was the only employee on site for another thirty minutes. The thought of being alone with a stranger, especially one this hot, started to give me heart palpitations. Cole must have sensed my panic, or perhaps the sheer look of bewilderment on my face, and immediately broke out in laughter. "You're looking at me like I'm holding two grenades. Everything all right?" He held up two tall foam cups from the coffee shop next to the museum. I recognized the label. My eyes went back and forth from his face to the coffee holder in his hands. *He brought me coffee?*

I was about to ask how he knew I worked here, and prayed Kendall would arrive early, when he set the coffee on the desk counter and gave me that silky smile, the same one that drove me wild inside at the wedding.

"Is Kendall not working today?" He looked around and I thought I saw a small blush creep up his neck.

*Kendall? What the heck? He's half her age, and she has kids!*

I cleared my throat, and my voice sounded hoarse when I spoke, "You're dating Kendall?" My eyes must have given away my shock and horror because he looked at me for a minute without saying anything and chuckled softly. *Now he's laughing at me?* I extended a nervous smile and waited for him to stop laughing, though secretly I didn't want him to. His dimples were cute as hell. *Damn it.*

He cleared his throat and shook his head, keeping an amused smirk on his face. "Kendall is my neighbor... well, she lives two doors down from me. She usually works on Wednesday mornings, and I told her I would drop off some coffee on my way to class."

Now it was my turn to look horrified as I stumbled through my next sentence, "So- you didn't ... you didn't know I work here?" My eyes shot back and forth between him and the lobby.

Cole gave another hearty laugh. "Sorry to disappoint you, but I am not a stalker. I've never seen you up here when I swing by on rare occasions, but I guess I got lucky today..." His rich eyes settled on mine and heat rose in my cheeks. He walked closer to my desk to set the two cups down on the ledge.

"Yeah, I guess it's your lucky day. Umm—err, you're right. I usually don't work on Wednesdays." I casually shuffled some papers from behind the desk and fell silent. I was at a loss for words and prayed my face wasn't as hot as I felt it getting. Neither of us spoke as I tried to form a sentence in my head, but nothing surfaced. This was now teetering on awkward, and I begged my brain to put together some words. *For the love of God!* I felt like a teenager being caught passing a note by the teacher and unable to speak when asked what was written on the scrap of paper.

Cole smirked and extended both hands out in front of him, finally breaking the silence. "So, you work here with Kendall? What a small world." He tilted his head at me. He was trying to make me feel comfortable and start a friendly conversation. If he noticed my flaming red face, he was doing a fantastic job of pretending I looked normal.

Now it was my turn to laugh. "Yeah, I must admit, that is so crazy you're her neighbor! You poor thing." I laughed at my own joke, knowing anyone who encountered Kendall probably knew her whole soap opera drama and couldn't escape her forty-five-minute, one-sided life story every time she ran into you.

Cole's eyes twinkled, but he was somber when he spoke, "Eh, she isn't that bad, just had some bad luck in the dating field. Her boys are great though. Sometimes I babysit them to give her some time off, since she has no one else and her loser ex rarely shows up as promised." Cole's eyes hardened at that last part, and I wondered what he knew that I didn't. I also melted a bit when he said he willingly offered to watch her twins. Seth wouldn't even play with his cousin's son, who always begged him to play football at family events. *Stop comparing your fiancé to a bartender you barely know!* What was wrong with me? Ever since the wedding I'd been dreaming about running into Cole again. Now it was really happening, and I was a bumbling idiot!

Cole checked his watch and frowned. "I need to head to class, but if Kendall isn't working today, feel free to have a cup of joe… on me." There was that dazzling smile again. At that instant I knew I was in trouble.

I offered a big smile in return as I envisioned the *physical* aspect of that statement – pouring coffee on Cole… and licking it off. *Oh my god, girl. Get a grip!* I knew Kendall was working the mid-morning shift with me, but I played dumb. Ever the graceful actress I was, I bent down and confirmed the name written on the calendar next to our phone, and to hide my red face again. *Kendall.*

"Actually, she is working with me today. I'll tell her you dropped off her coffee but had to leave." I smiled again and tried to ignore the butterflies swarming my stomach.

Cole tipped his head in the direction of the lobby and shuffled toward the door. "I'm at the coffee shop most mornings, and a few afternoons to study in between classes. If you ever want to meet up on a break or something..."

Heat rose in my face again as I fumbled for something to say. Anything! My eyes shifted around the room trying to find something to focus on besides him. I knew if I made direct contact with those warm, deep eyes, I'd be too weak to say no. Thankfully, before I could respond, he was gone.

I WALKED through the back door just after seven o'clock. Kendall managed to talk my ear off for thirty extra minutes. I was relieved I could finally escape when the front desk phone rang and she was forced to walk over and answer it. The duration of my shift was spent in a daze thinking about Cole and what a shock it was to see him again. Every time I thought about his gorgeous and inviting smile my cheeks grew warm, and I became paranoid that Kendall would get suspicious and call me out on my crush. I made a point of staying busy and mostly kept to myself for the rest of the day until Kendall cornered me right before I clocked out.

Once I pulled into our driveway, reality hit me. I lived with Seth. He was the man inside waiting for me to walk through the back door. My heart belonged with Seth. I was going to marry Seth. Cole was just a guy that I needed to put out of my mind. Besides, someone that cute probably had a hot girlfriend.

As I walked through the back door into the house, I saw Seth bent over at our small kitchen table, deep in thought. I also noticed my wedding binder was open and miscellaneous papers and business cards were strewn across the table. ESPN blared from the television in the living room, and I wondered, if for a brief moment, I was dreaming.

"Hey, hon. What's all this?" I slowly walked over to the

table, which now resembled a small paper war zone, and glanced over at his disaster of a mess.

"Oh, hey, babe… didn't even hear you come in! I know you've been stressed out working so much, so I wanted to do something nice for you. I figured I would get some of the wedding stuff done that you hadn't put a dent in." Seth smiled up at me like a puppy who had just done a trick and wanted a treat, or a compliment accompanied by a belly rub.

I cringed. I willed myself not to start screaming when I noticed that my wedding binder rested blissfully in the middle of the table with the spine open, and different tabs were loosely scattered on the table and NOT in the carefully designed and organized binder the way I had painfully spent hours on end creating and perfecting.

*Breathe, Bethany. Stay calm. He isn't worth the jail time!*

"Seth, what the hell are you doing?" My voice rose as I started to collect what remained of my wedding binder from the messy table.

Seth scrunched his brows together and looked perplexed, then annoyed.

"I was trying to help you move this wedding planning along. I mean, my mom is concerned about a few things, and I told her about your long, unfinished to-do list and she thought I needed to step in since you were going too slow. *Someone* needs to get things moving along." His comments enraged me. As if I were sitting around in my spare time eating bon bons and enjoying online shopping. I had a full-time job, and I also cooked and cleaned—something he knew nothing about!

He acted like he was doing me a favor, and it irritated me even more.

"Well, maybe your MOTHER should mind her own business. I'm marrying you—not her! Did you also tell her that I've been doing *everything* while you sit around and do nothing but complain and criticize? The cake for example –"

"Oh yeah—about that. I paid for the cake." He grinned at

me with that stupid puppy dog look again. I think I felt my eyeballs bulge out of their sockets for a mere minute before settling back in their rightful place. My heartbeat picked up speed, and I felt like someone sucker punched me in the face.

"SETH! How could you pay for the cake when we haven't even agreed on the cake flavor or the design yet?" I was furious. He was ruining my plans! All the Hallmark and romcom movies had the guy and the girl tasting the cakes together. There was always a whole montage scene of funny and cute cake eating with a Maroon Five or Train song playing throughout. The cake decorator would make a big show and bring out multiple cake displays, and the couple would swoon over or dispute the options—together—then laugh... while eating cake! I wanted that! Who attends their own wedding without seeing or tasting their own cake?!

"What's the big deal? A cake is a cake. I told her we would come by for a tasting, told her our wedding colors, and gave her full reign to come up with an idea. She *is* a cake designer. I mean, it is her job. I'm sure she can handle it." Seth shook his head like I was being the crazy one and got up and walked over to the kitchen to grab a Gatorade from the fridge.

*What's the big deal? It's our wedding cake—it is a BIG deal!* I was so upset and hurt that he was treating this like our wedding was just another typical day. It should be special! Not to mention all the hard work I had put in to get so much done for it. My eye caught the end of the kitchen counter, and I saw that the two wedding envelopes for his Uncle Fletcher and Aunt Louise were still waiting on addresses that Seth had yet to provide me.

I gathered the remaining loose papers still on the table and grabbed my binder to head upstairs to our bedroom. Tears threatened to spill over any minute, and I wanted to be alone. I raced up the stairs and took refuge in our bedroom, where I sprawled myself out on our bed and let the water works flow.

Twenty minutes later I could still hear the television from

downstairs, and I realized that Seth wasn't coming up to talk to me or that he even realized how upset I was. Was this the life I wanted to live from here on out? Could I really be with a guy who didn't see the big deal about choosing our wedding cake together and thought I was overreacting? What else would he decide for us without consulting me first?

I rubbed my eyes. I was exhausted and having a bad day. Between work and wedding planning, maybe I was just overly stressed. The wedding was two months away. I couldn't call it off. Everything was basically paid for. Plus, how would I ever start over at this stage of my life? I decided I would calm myself down and then apologize to Seth in the morning for overreacting when he was just trying to help.

That night I went to bed and dreamt about walking down the aisle. Everything was perfect. I had my beautiful dress on, the church was full of our friends and family, and up at the altar was the priest standing next to a gorgeous vintage, ivory-frosted cake waiting for me. I smiled as I cut into the first slice and when I looked up from the cake, I saw that Cole was standing next to me in a crisp black tuxedo.

# Chapter 12

**Welcome back, Bethany! Would you like to continue where you left off?**
**Great! Have fun journaling!**

This morning I couldn't shake the feeling of wondering if Henry O'Doole is still in Pittsburgh, or even online for that matter. I haven't thought of him in ages. I know he ended up transferring to another school system outside our city in sixth grade when his parents decided to sell their house and upgrade to a bigger one. I never saw him again.

Henry was the first and last crush I had until high school, specifically my junior year. That's when Shane McCoy came into my life. He was an old soul and a bad boy. We met in art class, and I think I drooled all over myself the first time I saw him behind an easel. Jet black hair, crisp blue eyes, and my all-time weakness ... dimples.

Of course, I was too shy to ever approach him, other than asking him for an art supply here and there. I knew my parents would ship me off to boarding school if I ever came home dating a guy like Shane.

I stopped journaling for a minute and wondered if I

should type his name in the search bar and see if he popped up.

I knew I was about to jump down the rabbit hole and do what most brides-to-be should never *ever* do: I was going to Facebook to stalk another man. I mean, technically I was just curious to see whatever happened to Henry. After having that crazy dream last night about Cole, I ended up dreaming about Henry—of all people! I tried super hard to fall back asleep and have sweet dreams about Seth, but all I could think about was our stupid fight. His snoring didn't help either. *I guess it wouldn't do much harm to see what Shane's up to as well.*

"Get a grip, Bethany!"

It was bad enough I was even thinking about one guy, now I was adding to the parade? Henry, Shane... I couldn't stalk Cole because I didn't know his last name. *OMG. What the hell is wrong with me?!*

Getting married was turning me into a lunatic. Before I lost my nerve, I bit the bullet as I held my breath and typed his name into the search bar. My heart was beating a mile a minute and my palms felt clammy. I hit enter and squeezed my eyes shut. A second later a whole page populated, full of the name *Henry O'Doole*. I even had taglines to filter further: *all, posts, people, groups, events...* the list went on. I selected *People* and then skimmed the bios next to each picture before my mouth dropped. There was a photo of a golden lab next to two young children—a boy and a girl. In the background was a glimpse of a lovely brick house. *Pittsburgh, PA. Chiropractor. Dr. Henry O'Doole.*

No way! Was that him? The other names were from cities and states outside of Pennsylvania. He was the only one with a Pittsburgh address. I couldn't believe my eyes. Of course, he was married! I smiled for a moment, wondering when he had decided girls stopped having cooties? I tried searching for Shane's name. Hell—at this point I was already in too deep. Might as well!

Unfortunately, nothing popped up for him, but I had no idea where he was living or whatever happened to him after high school. I typed in Seth's name. He hardly ever went on social media unless it was to post something about the Steelers. His page had been inactive since April. Finding exactly what I expected—nothing—I hopped back over to my journal tab to update it.

I can't believe Henry is married with kids. Why does it seem like everyone is married with children and I can't even get Seth to agree to one child? He would rather deal with the stress of owning a dog—a puppy, no less—than raise a child with me! I feel like I'm coming to terms with saying goodbye to my childhood fantasy of being a mother and shutting the door on my future family for good once I walk down that aisle to Seth.

Sometimes life doesn't pan out the way you want it to. I have a good life, a man who loves me and wants to marry me. Maybe that's enough. The grass isn't always greener on the other side.

I closed out my journal and stared at Henry's Facebook profile for a few more minutes before logging out and heading to the kitchen to pour myself a glass of wine. I tipped the cup back and toasted myself, "Here's to your life, Bethany, whatever it's meant to look like."

The second week of September my parents invited all of us over for Sunday dinner. It was more of a Welcome Home party for Josh and Ellie, who'd just returned from their honeymoon to Italy. The only Tour of Italy Seth and I could afford would be up the street at our local Olive Garden for $12.99.

My mother decided to make *vegetarian* lasagna, since Ellie didn't eat meat. How does that even qualify as food? Of course, Seth didn't like spinach, so we also had to have regular spaghetti for him. Seth didn't eat anything green—salads, green peppers, cucumbers, spinach. He had the appetite of a preschooler. It was another big difference between us. Whereas I ate just about anything, Seth had a small window of foods he would even consider tasting. Unless he was drunk, of course, then he ate anything—like mushrooms!

Seth and I were the last ones to arrive at my parents' house. We pulled in behind my brother's black Audi A7 that glistened in my parents' driveway. I was shocked he still had this car considering he was always trading his vehicle in for the bigger, better, newer model. Shouldn't someone who's having a baby invest in a more practical vehicle, like a mini-van? Or an SUV?

We walked through the back door, which led into my parents' kitchen, and saw everyone sitting around the table looking at photo books. My mother didn't even look up when we entered. She just threw her hand in the air to wave us over and then went right back to flipping pages in the photo book, studying each one intently as she beamed. I rolled my eyes. *Great!* Tonight was going to be all about the two love birds again before we even sat down to eat. Seth walked over to my parents and shook my dad's hand and acknowledged my mom, who was now audibly oohing and ahhing over one of the honeymoon photos before sitting down at one of the empty chairs around the table. Seth looked up at me expectantly. "Beth, come sit down. Looks like they're just looking at the honeymoon photos. I've never been to Italy, but I've heard it's absolutely amazing," Seth said to no one specific, as he picked up one of the smaller photo books that had already been viewed by everyone else and started to flip through the pages. I grunted and slowly sunk down into the last empty seat next to Seth. Ellie's belly was finally starting to protrude, but she still barely looked pregnant. I didn't think it was safe to even fly during pregnancy, so I was surprised her doctor let her travel out of the United States.

My mother finally closed the last of the books and looked up at us. "Josh and Ellie were just telling us how spectacular Italy was. Oh, I hope your father and I can go one day when we retire." My mother lovingly looked over at my father, who

chuckled and nodded in agreement. My parents made rela-
tionships look so easy. I had never witnessed a fight between
the two of them in all the years I lived under their roof. My
father always seemed to do whatever it took to make my
mother happy. He never seemed to care about his own needs
as long as hers were met. Every night, for as long as I could
remember, my father would get home from work and then
take over cooking for my mother in the kitchen. He loved to
cook and always doted on my mother. She would retire to the
kitchen chair and he would bring her tea (her favorite evening
drink) and leftover biscuits while he finished cooking our
nightly dinner. I always loved watching them together in the
kitchen. Even though they both worked full time, he always
put her first.

"How was the food there?" I tried to make polite small
talk. I knew how good the food was in Italy. *Everyone* knows
how ridiculously delicious Italian food is. My mother got up to
set the table and get the food ready, and Josh immediately
launched into a twenty-minute speech about their pizza and
wine. Seth hung on every word that came out of my brother's
mouth, especially considering pizza was his favorite food
group. Actually, it was his only food group.

I tuned them out while we all passed my mother's lasagna
around and loaded our dishes up with what she lovingly
referred to as "the Bowers' Sunday Feast."

After dinner, my mother made me help clear the dishes
and reset the table for dessert. I was ready to call it a night,
but my mother refused to let us leave without a slice of her
homemade apple pie. I had to admit, her pie was delicious,
good enough to make me suffer through a few more of Josh
and Ellie's honeymoon stories. If I heard one more, *"Oh,
Bethany, you guys just have to visit Italy! Your life will never be the
same!"* I would waste all that delicious apple pie by throwing it
up all over my shoes.

After everyone had a slice of warm pie on their plates,

Josh cleared his throat and got everyone's attention. *Oh brother. Now what was their new announcement?*

Ellie beamed and smiled at Josh as she rubbed her belly, which was now slightly swollen and looked like mine did after I overate. I still had a hard time believing she was carrying a baby in there, considering she was the skinniest pregnant woman I had ever seen. "We decided on a name and wanted to share it with you all!" Ellie smiled, and my mother gasped and clapped her hands in anticipation. My father leaned forward balancing his elbows on the table (something my mother hated but at this point hadn't even noticed) and cradled his head in his hands, which were folded together, and nodded for Ellie to go on.

Ellie and Josh smiled at one another, and I rolled my eyes in annoyance. The entire dinner was spent talking about them, as always.

Ellie squeezed Josh's hand and spoke in a higher-than-normal voice, "We decided to name our baby girl Tinsley McPherson Bowers!" She squealed at her own announcement, and my parents clapped and got up to hug them both. Everyone was tearing up, even my father. I sat frozen in my chair with my mouth open at the scene playing out in front of me.

"What a beautiful name!" My mother gushed as she continued to tightly hug Ellie, wiping away a tear.

"I know! Isn't it pretty? It was my great grandmother's maiden name, and I thought it would be nice to use for our daughter." Ellie continued to rub her belly. Seth smacked my arm and whispered, "You're being weird. Say something to them."

I cleared my throat and hoarsely congratulated them on their name. I felt my own eyes start to water, but not out of happiness.

Seth smacked Josh's back and hugged Ellie as he complimented them on their news.

After everyone sat back down, I wondered how long we would have to sit there and talk about the baby. I wanted to get out of there. The fact that my brother got married first (at an amazing venue, no less), was going to become a father, and just got back from a three-week-long trip to Europe tugged at my heartstrings a little too much. I needed time to process all of this.

# Chapter 13

I checked my watch one more time for good measure. It was now fifteen minutes past ten o'clock, and I was settled into one of the front tables located inside the coffee shop adjacent to my job. It was one of the perks of working at the museum. I was off today but Cole didn't know that, unless Kendall had opened her big mouth. I was half expecting to see him hunched over one of the tables with his textbook in hand, already deep in thought, when I walked in. Then I could surprise him by walking up to his table and feigning shock. I would joke about it being a small world and would offer to buy him his favorite latte. *Although, he did tell you he frequents this place a few mornings before class,* my no-good conscience reminded me. I scoffed at my inner voice and quieted her by taking a sip of my now-lukewarm coffee.

I had arrived about thirty minutes before, book in hand and ready to have some *me* time. I looked down at my worn cover of *A Tree Grows in Brooklyn* and opened the spine to the spot containing my bookmark. I was halfway through the book and still hadn't decided if I liked it or not. Every time I tried to get into it, my mind wandered to my upcoming wedding, especially my wedding jitters, and my niece-to-be. I was determined to finish this book and pull myself together. A smile crossed my lips as I started reading the first paragraph. Seth had found this book at a garage sale that his parents' neighbor had last summer. He spent a whole seventy-five cents on it and surprised me after dinner later that night. He knew my passion for reading and figured I would be happy with his purchase.

Now we were purchasing a ten-thousand-dollar wedding together and vowing to honor one another through thick and thin, in sickness and in health. I wish I could find the small print that discussed the return policy on a wedding. Oh yeah. There was none! How could I spend the rest of my life with a guy who was content with plain 'ol vanilla cake? All he wanted was the standard lifestyle, the bare minimum. When I made my special homemade pizza dough, all he ever wanted on his half was mozzarella cheese. No toppings, no special cheese blend, nothing that screamed special. Just cheese. Just *plain*.

"Ahem… that must be one interesting book you're reading there."

I knew that voice! I felt the redness creep up my neck trying to find my cheeks. I looked up to find Cole's warm and comforting eyes staring down at me. A lopsided smile greeted me. *Dang it! I did it again!* I looked up at his dimples protruding from both sides of his perfectly round mouth and felt my cheeks flare up. Dimples did it for me every time.

I cleared my throat. "Cole! What are you doing here? Don't you have class?"

I invited him to sit, and he moved his way towards the other chair across from mine. I quickly took a sip of my now-cold coffee to distract him from directly staring at my red face. I felt myself gag as the cold liquid tried to find its way down my throat. *Note to self: never ever try to chug cold coffee! Nasty!* Cole patted his book bag, that I hadn't even noticed until now, hanging from his right side.

"I have some stuff to do before class. Figured I would hide

out here with a nice cold caramel latte—for a sugar high—so I don't fall asleep while reading." He flashed his dimples at me again and my heart fluttered.

One of the baristas came around to wipe down a table next to us and grinned when she saw Cole. "Well, look who it is. My favorite customer! Have you decided to put those dimples to good use and come work here part time yet?"

The dark-haired girl was clearly flirting with him, and it made me angry. How did she know if we were together or not? I mean, clearly we weren't, but she didn't know that! Cole let out a hearty laugh. "Raquel here has been trying forever to get me to put on an apron." I smiled and gave him a puzzled look. "I'm here quite a lot, and I can probably make every-thing on the menu without help, but nothing beats the money I make bartending on the weekends." He shook his shoulders in surrender, laughed, and sat back in his chair. Raquel doubled over with laughter. *Why doesn't she just throw herself on him already?*

"Want your regular, sir?" she teased him with a flirty sparkle in her eyes. I was sure she was also licking her lips at his deep carved dimples that seemed to get deeper and more prominent every time he spoke.

"Absolutely, boss!" he chuckled back. The barista playfully smacked his shoulder, and he feigned pain. I was starting to feel like a third wheel on a mock date that I set up!

She finished wiping the table down and then waved as she walked back to the front of the counter to start his order.

"She really likes you," I blurted out before I even realized what I was saying.

Cole's eyes sparkled and he teased me with a half-smile. "Is that so?"

"Why are you laughing at me? I'm a girl. I know these things." I sounded like a jealous girlfriend.

"She's actually dating another guy who works here. She's just a very flirty person. In fact, I know all the employees because I'm here so often. I'm what you call a 'regular.'" He made bunny ears with both his hands as he quoted his last word.

Raquel swung by as if on cue and delivered his latte with an abundance of whipped cream on top. When the front door chimed, she looked up and immediately began waving and smiling to a tall, dark-haired guy who smiled back warmly at her.

"Logan! How are you, my love? Take a seat. I'll bring your drink right out." She smiled back at us one last time then made her way to the front of the shop.

Cole chuckled, proving his point that Raquel was *not* hitting on him.

"Ugh. Fine. She is *suupper* friendly. My woman radar failed me miserably." Now I felt like an idiot. I laughed and rolled my eyes.

"Told ya so." He continued to laugh with his eyes. There was something almost comforting in his stare.

Heat rose in my cheeks again. *Don't look directly at his dimples!*

I cleared my throat and changed the subject. "So, what are you majoring in?"

# Chapter 14

Being friends with Heidi meant knowing each episode of *Sex and the City* inside and out. I remember when we first became friends (outside of being coworkers). She would constantly reference something Samantha, Carrie, Charlotte, or Miranda did in an episode, and I would nonchalantly agree how funny or inappropriate it was, even though I had no idea who these women were. Finally, she caught on that I had never seen an episode. I didn't realize why it was a big deal until she called me over for a *SATC* marathon. I figured it would be like a typical "marathon" with friends where you drank too much and let conversation or gossip rule the night, completely forgetting the whole reason for the girl's night in the first place. Nope. Not with Heidi, and not with *Sex and the City*. After season one I was hooked. I honestly hated the first few episodes, but I had faith in Heidi when she promised I would be obsessed with the rest of the seasons. Sarah Jessica Parker grew on me.

I was beginning to feel like I was reliving Carrie and Aidan's story in season 4 of "Just Say Yes" where Carrie's apartment is going co-op, so Aidan proposes he buy it, and she wonders if he would be her landlord or her boyfriend. Then she finds this hideous engagement ring when he's taking a shower, and she throws up.

As much as I loved Seth, I was beginning to feel like throwing up thinking about a future with him. But I kept chalking it up to nerves.

When Aidan finally proposes, he has this gorgeous ring that he swapped out for the ugly one, and Carrie is shocked and relieved.

I looked down at my gorgeous engagement ring and felt proud that Seth picked it out all by himself. *He truly knows and loves me, and I think I need—no I owe it to him—to make this work.* I decided I would have a serious talk with him over dinner that night. Thankfully, it was Friday, which meant ordering pizza. Since my brother's engagement party, Seth had taken a liking to red wine, which was both good and bad. Good because now I had someone to split the bottle with. Bad because he was still picky about which brands he would drink. I lucked out at the grocery store the previous week and scored a few bottles of a red blend mix that were on sale. I poured us both a generous glass and set a tray of BBQ wings in the middle of the table. I knew Seth loved wings and he had to work over-time that day, which meant that he would be ravenous when he got home. I had the pizza staying warm in the oven. I heard Seth's car pull up in the driveway.

I pulled the pizza out and had just put a few pieces on his plate when he walked in.

"Hey, babe. This looks great. I'm starving. Oh sweet! You even ordered wings. You're the best!" He gave me a quick kiss on the cheek and sat down, already picking up a piece of pizza before I even sat down to join him.

"How was your day?" I felt proud that my surprise was a hit and he had hot food waiting for him after a long day. *Look at me playing the wife role already.*

Seth grunted a few times, which meant there was nothing much to say about his mundane job. I took a bite of pizza and washed it down with the red wine. I let it dance on my tongue as a sliver of sunlight came through the window shade and hit my ring, making it sparkle even more. I raised my left hand in front of my face to admire it.

"I love this ring. You did a good job picking it out." I smiled as I gave Seth the compliment, knowing he would be impressed with himself.

Seth had half a chicken wing in his mouth and wiped some sauce that crept up on the side of his cheek. He squinted at the ring then took another bite of his now-meatless wing and followed it with a sip of wine.

"Oh yeah, it's pretty. And it was expensive. Marcy picked it out, which was probably better than the ring I originally selected." He reached out to pour himself more wine.

I blinked and looked at him like he had just slapped me.

"Marcy…?" I let her name hang there in between us while I tried to rack my brain for a face that matched that name.

Seth looked at me like I had asked him about the weather. "Yeah. Marcy. She's one of our dispatchers. When I told her I wanted to propose to you but had no idea what type of ring to get or what you would like, she offered to go with me. I'm glad she did. Obviously, she did a great job. You love the ring." There was that lopsided puppy dog look again, like he was waiting for praise.

There was a loud whooshing noise in my ears, and I felt like I was going to throw up but remained seated at the table. My heart was doing this super-fast drumbeat, and I was bracing myself to experience a real-life anxiety attack any minute.

The last two years were one big lie. Seth didn't know anything about me! He didn't even pick out the most important symbol of our future. Some woman named Marcy did. I had to ask him about this. His response would determine my next move. This moment was everything. I had to be brave. I had to finally stick up for myself.

I cleared my throat. "Hey, Seth?"

"What's up?" He was finishing another wing and licking his fingers to get the remaining sauce off.

I willed myself not to cry, no matter what the answer was. I folded my hands in front of me and looked at him expectantly.

"Do you want a boy or a girl?"

Seth stopped eating and tilted his head as if in thought.

*Ok, this could be promising.* He didn't immediately say anything, so I repeated the question.

"I figured we could get a boy first and see how that works out." He gulped some more wine and took another slice of pizza from the box and shoved it in his mouth. *Such a caveman.*

Puzzled, I looked at him. "Get a boy? What are you talking about? You want to adopt?"

Seth looked at me like I had five heads suddenly.

"Bethany, I was talking about the gender of the dog we would get. Didn't you say you wanted to move forward with a dog? I thought we decided that was our game plan."

"I want a real baby!" I blurted out. *Shit!* I didn't mean to say it that way.

Seth chewed the remaining pizza in his mouth, patted his lips with a napkin and sadly shook his head.

"Babe, we went over this. I don't want a baby. Ever. I thought you understood that. It's not you. It's me."

*It's now or never. You have to tell him the truth!* My brain was yelling at me. All my fears were coming true. This wasn't going to be happily ever after. I was going to live a lie for the rest of my life if I didn't tell him right now. *Just say it, Bethany! This is the rest of your life we're talking about!*

"I want a baby. I want to be a mother. If I can't have that with you, then I need to find it with someone else." I didn't even recognize my own voice in that moment. I was finally being honest with myself in front of Seth. A guy I was willing to do anything for, except give up being a mother. It was my first dream as a little girl, and I wanted to make it come true as a woman. If not with Seth, then with someone else who shared that dream.

Seth looked both appalled and aggravated as I told him this. He got out of his chair and paced our small kitchen area, running a hand through his thick mane and shaking his head back and forth. He would stop then start the process again and did this for a full two minutes before quickly turning and pointing his finger at me. I could see the hurt in his eyes.

"Beth, we're getting married in less than two months. What are you talking about? You don't just end a marriage over a non-existent baby!" He threw his hands in the air. To him, I was crazy for wanting and craving something he had no desire to ever want or crave. He didn't understand that I saw marriage as the next step in creating a family—our family—who would then one day create their own family. "Seth, I get that you think you don't want kids right now, but I'm sure you'll change your mind one day. I know you're not into other people's kids much, but if we had our own—"

The look in his eyes stopped me mid-sentence. "Beth, I. Don't. Want. Kids. Ever. I know that's probably hard to hear, but it's the truth. I have to be honest with you. I thought you knew this about me."

I got up and took his hands in mine. I knew this would be our last time to ever touch and be this close to one another. The tears found their way to my eyes and I didn't even acknowledge them. I let them flood my face knowing that they deserved this escape as much as I did. I was standing up for that little innocent girl, who at age seven planned her future with a husband, dog, and two kids. It had been a long time since I had allowed that little girl to lead my future and follow my dreams.

"I love you, Seth, with all of my heart. But I love the little girl in me more. I want to have a baby, and I will never be able to forgive myself if I deny myself that right. I have to at least try to make my dream happen, with or without you." I didn't even bother to wipe my tears, and I saw that Seth was still just staring at me like I was speaking a foreign language.

Silence filled the space between us for what seemed like forever, until finally Seth pulled me in and held me close as we both cried and grieved for the life we would never have. Soon, there was nothing left to say but goodbye. Finally, he pulled away and said in the saddest voice I've ever heard, "I'll call all the guests and tell them the wedding's off. Take your time finding another place to live."

*That's right.* This was Seth's house. He wasn't kicking me out, really, but I didn't feel right staying there any longer than I needed to. It was time for a clean slate.

My heart sank as he continued, "I'm going to a friend's house tonight, so you can have some time alone. I think we both might need that right now."

He softly closed the door behind him, and the tears flooded my cheeks once again. I really wanted to call Heidi at that moment, but I needed some time to process everything that had just happened. I pulled an entire cheesecake out of the fridge, poured a glass of wine, and settled in for a self-loathing night complete with a binge fest of *Sex and the City*. This was as close to my bestie as I was going to get tonight.

# Chapter 15

I called Heidi the next day, after Seth left early to play golf with his father and uncle. I knew he hated the sport, but he was trying to give me time to myself, for which I was grateful. Heidi answered on the third ring, sounding out of breath.

I could already feel the tears trying to escape my eyes, and I willed myself not to cry. This was going to be the hardest weekend. I had to start packing up all the engagement gifts to send them back, some of which we never even had the chance to open.

My parents, Josh, and even Ellie all seemed truly upset and shell shocked when I called them last night to explain that Seth and I were calling off the wedding. My mother said it was nonsense to pack up anything our side of the family gave us because she knew how our family operated. It was Operation Bowers. They would all feel guilty if I sent back their gifts, knowing I could benefit from most of them once I moved into my own place. My extended family was much bigger than Seth's side, so the majority of gifts came from my family and our friends and co-workers. We received beautiful pots and pans, dinnerware, bedding sets, and much more. I tried to tell my mother that I would be mortified to keep anything, but she went right into one of her lectures, so I just gave up and agreed to keep everything.

"Hey, girl! What's up?" Heidi sounded like she had run a marathon before answering the phone. I guess packing can be a real workout. I made a mental note for when I started my packing process.

"You might want to sit for this." I warned her knowing that she would continue to stand. The thought made me laugh because I realized she didn't have any furniture left. Today they were driving to Cleveland and officially leaving Pittsburg behind. Everyone in my life that I loved or cared about was now gone. I was all alone.

"Har har, smart ass." Heidi cackled on the other line. I could hear her taping a box up, probably her gigantic Keurig. Leave it to Heidi to make her final cup of coffee on her last morning.

"I ended things with Seth last night." I was surprisingly calm when I had said it out loud that morning. I felt at peace with my decision knowing that I was doing the right thing after all.

"What? Why? What happened?" Heidi started talking a mile a minute and I had to talk over her multiple times before she shut up. God, I was going to miss this girl!

"You were right. I want a baby more than anything, and Seth doesn't ever want that with me or anyone. So, I ended it. It was the hardest thing ever. I'm mortified that we have to tell everyone the wedding is off. We are out so much money. But mostly, my heart just hurts right now." I think I was out of tears because I had cried so much the night before.

"Why didn't you tell me sooner?" Heidi softened and went into her good-friend spiel of how I will find myself again and fall in love again, and it will be with the right guy. It was everything I didn't want to hear before but knew I had to believe now. I knew I had to be strong, even if I didn't want to be.

"I think I already found someone," I said sheepishly.

"WHAT?? Whoa, girly! Back up and start from the beginning!" Heidi was floored when I back peddled to the night of Josh's wedding and I told her about Cole and how I ran into him at the coffee shop (she didn't need to know every detail).

I told her about Ellie and Josh naming their baby girl and how excited they looked and felt, and I knew that night that I would never be full of love if I didn't have that piece of my life. I knew that all the speeches Heidi always gave me were right and I was just avoiding the truth. It was easier to live in denial. I was content with my life, but I wasn't happy.

I knew if I was really in love with Seth and really happy with myself then I wouldn't be hung up on some random, good-looking stranger. I wouldn't be seeking him out and getting all fluttery when he talked or looked at me. I wouldn't wonder if he wanted a family or if he liked kids. Someone in a happy relationship doesn't wonder that about other people.

Heidi and I talked for another hour before I realized the time. I knew I had to get some moving boxes and start making progress before Seth came home. My parents told me I could move back in with them until I found a place. As much as I never wanted to do that again, I realized I needed to. I had to save up money and find a place. Just thinking about it made me depressed.

I told Heidi as much. I knew she had to get on the road, as they had so much unpacking to do, and Heidi wanted to get a job sooner than later once they settled in Cleveland.

"I have to tell you something, Bethany. I was going to tell you when you first called, but I realized it should wait. I've been dying this whole time!" I could hear the excitement in her voice but also hesitation.

"Well, tell me! God knows I've talked your ear off the last hour." I poured myself a cup of coffee and sat down at the table. *We've had so many meals at this table together, and now I'm ending it having my final cup of coffee alone.* I sighed then refocused on Heidi.

"... Colin and I are thrilled. It's going to be the best surprise ever once we get home to his family later today! We are already picking out names. Totally thrilled and I'm sorry I haven't said anything, but we wanted to be sure this time. But this is it. This time is real. We're having a baby!"

Coffee sputtered out my nose and all over the table. I inhaled before I choked.

I felt my heart pick up speed, like it did the other night with Seth. I knew a monumental moment was about to take place. The fight-or-flight response kicked in, and I could either lose my best friend or accept the situations in my life for what they were—*signs* and hopefully *hope* to show me that I, too, could achieve this happiness—eventually.

"Congratulations! I'm so happy for you!" Tears pricked at my eyes as my voice cracked, and I felt both heartache and joy simultaneously.

"Oh my god, I am such a shit! I should have waited a few more days or weeks to say anything, given everything you are dealing with now." I heard Heidi sob on the other line, and it brought even more tears to my already-swollen face.

"Heidi, do not feel bad about being pregnant! This is your moment, and I really am happy for you and Colin! It's not your fault that I chose to end my engagement because I was in such deep denial that the guy I was going to spend my life with didn't want the same things I did! It's truly a dream and an honor to become a parent. You have every right to be excited!" My voice faltered as I got up on my soapbox to preach about the Facts of Life—something Heidi was usually much better at, given her very outspoken Italian roots, which went without saying, *"Here's my opinion whether you want it or not."*

Heidi had gone through so much when she was pregnant before, then found out it was an ectopic pregnancy and the nightmare that she endured through that period of time was unimaginable. I would never feel angry at her finally catching a break and having a successful pregnancy.

I did feel anger at myself and my stupid denial that I really thought I was in love with a man who was content to build his life around the Steelers, take-out food, a wife at his beck and call, and a dog... but no kids, ever. I had allowed myself to settle for someone and live their life and their dreams while discarding mine. That wasn't a relationship. I set the precedent early on that my needs could be negotiated. But a baby wasn't like negotiating pepperoni on a pizza. I should have realized that I wasn't ever going to change Seth's mind about becoming a parent. I thought loving someone would be enough, but I love me more. I love my dreams and my future to raise my offspring more than playing house with a man who would never want anything more from me. I didn't want to settle. Life was too short to settle for the bare minimum. I didn't want a vanilla life.

I was going to channel my inner child (that sassy, fearless girl) and put myself out there again and be bold and brave. I was going to find that dream man who would give me my dream children and dogs and the white picket fence (because of the dogs), and we would order pizza that had lots of toppings on it... and both pick vanilla as our least favorite flavor.

# Epilogue
## 3 MONTHS LATER

I smothered my dark hair for the hundredth time before Cole looked over at me and grabbed my hand, giving it a firm squeeze. I was trying to relax and breathe, but we were on our way to meet his parents for the first time, and I was a hot mess. Today was a huge day. First, I was meeting my boyfriend's (yes! I was dating a replica of Tom Cruise back in the Top Gun days) parents over brunch. Then we were going over to Josh and Ellie's house to see my newly born niece. Today was a big day!

"I'm fine. Totally fine." I looked over at Cole and into his scrumptious coffee-colored eyes, which always seemed to be dancing with excitement. I exhaled and leaned back into the passenger seat of his Jeep Cherokee. The last few months seemed like a dream - one I didn't want to wake from.

Cole chuckled and lifted my hand to his mouth where he gifted it with a quick kiss. My stomach still did little summersaults every time he touched me.

"My parents are going to love you. And my mom is beyond thrilled that I'm finally introducing them to someone and not having a secret love affair with a hot Italian behind closed doors." He winked as he said this, and I had to laugh out loud. Cole told me his parents were constantly asking him about his love life and why he hadn't brought anyone around. He was the youngest of three and the only one still single.

My heart did that ridiculous flutter again, and I felt myself blushing at the thought that *I* was the girl he was comfortable bringing around. I immediately sucked in a huge breath, and at the same time Cole read my mind by saying, "No, my siblings will not be crashing this brunch. Trust me. I threatened them all with their deepest darkest secrets I've been keeping for such occasions." I slightly relaxed but still felt like I was going to throw up all over my brand-new outfit that I bought for the "meet the boyfriend's parents and hope they like me" occasion. An outfit was everything. It gave so many clues to someone's personality.

I wanted to look put together without giving off a "trying too hard" vibe. I had tried on what felt like twenty outfits when Heidi and I were shopping at Nordstrom—her favorite store—during my last visit to Cleveland. I guess her pregnancy hormones had started kicking in because she let out a huff and flung a rose-colored cashmere sweater at me over the stall as the dressing-room attendant chuckled at our charade. Before I even had the garment over my body, I knew it was the right one. It screamed, *"Nice to meet you. I really have a crush on your son, but I am being respectful about it."* I stepped out of the stall feeling like a million bucks, then rubbed her almost-non-existent baby belly and said, "Guess your maternal instincts are kicking in already." We both laughed and an hour later I was leaving with the perfect look for the new perfect man.

A minute later Cole pulled into the restaurant parking spot. This was really happening. I took another shaky breath and forced myself to smile. I was meeting this man's parents, not going to the gas chamber! I could totally do this.

"Beth, my parents are going to love you. I want them to meet the girl who makes me laugh and who's responsible for me gaining a few pounds." He patted his rock-solid abs as if anyone could even tell if he really did gain two pounds, let alone more. It was true that I had been steadily feeding this man as he finished his last semester that would earn him a bachelor's degree to teach third graders! I occasionally ran into Kendall, but she was now growing on me and I couldn't even be that annoyed with her anymore. I was in love again... okay, very much *liking* a man again. I could cut Kendall some slack.

I smiled at Cole, imagining everything my new life could be. I had a new man, with whom I shared a lot of common interests, and new goals that I could actually see myself achieving. I finally realized how lucky I was that my brother did get married first, and I was starting to believe in the whole "everything happens for a reason" bit.

With my new (but probably short-lived) confidence, I grabbed Cole's hand and pulled him forward towards the door. "Let's meet these amazing parents of yours." I realized that my smile was truly sincere.

"C'mon, let's do this. Then we can go see that adorable little niece of yours." Cole got out and came around to my side of the passenger door and opened it for me. Once again my heart took flight, and I knew this was my path. I smiled and offered a soft but confident nod. "Let's do this," I said as I took his hand.

THE END

# Acknowledgments

First and foremost, I want to thank all of you who took the time to read my book. I was so excited to jump back into author mode and finish this book that I started five years ago - before Mommyhood took over! I knew I always wanted to finish it, and I finally got serious about it. So, thank you for believing in me and investing your time to read this. I hope you enjoyed it!

I sincerely want to thank my husband, who has been through every up and down with me and has always encouraged me to chase my dreams. He knows I am a fanatic about reading books, and I will literally choose reading over socializing any day, but he also knew how important publishing this book was to me. When I told him I was ready to get serious about finishing it, he was completely on board. He is my rock and the best husband and daddy, and I am immensely blessed by all the bonuses he brings into my life. Even when I don't always tell him these things, I hope he knows how amazing he is.

Special thanks to my amazing and super-talented editor Traci Sanders. Seriously, in my next life I hope to come back as a gifted editor! She really made my vision of my story and the characters come to life. I am so grateful I kept her information from all those years ago and that she agreed to work with me (for real this time!) because my story wouldn't be anywhere near as amazing without her!

Thank you to Magic Machine Designs for adding text to my book cover to really make it stand out. I love it!

Misty Snyder, thank you for being my biggest supporter!! I will be sending you a signed paperback as soon as I go to print! Ha ha.

Jen Alexinas, who I have always deemed my "Charlotte York." I will never give up trying to make a reader out of you!

I drew my inspiration of Bethany and Heidi from my real-life friends and their real-life situations that every woman faces at some point. I hope that my readers were able to connect to one or both of these characters.

I originally wrote this book from the POV of Bethany and Heidi, but then I ditched that entire writing style after I wrote most of the book and realized that the vibe I wanted wasn't there. At the time, I was actually going through the aftermath of losing my first child from an ectopic pregnancy, and I thought that writing about it would help me overcome some of that heartache. And it did. Because of that, I chose to scrap the two POVs and focus strictly on Bethany. So, that did take some time to rework, and then in between all that I got pregnant again and had a beautiful and healthy baby boy, and then another gorgeous boy not long after that. My family is now complete, and I chose to put my strength in raising my family. However, the dream of publishing this book never left my heart. Now my goal is complete.

Thank you to all who pushed me along the way to not give up.

Printed in Great Britain
by Amazon